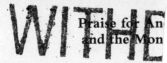

"Wit and delicacy and the fast-cut timing of farce play across the surface . . . but what keeps it from frothing into mere intellectual charm is the persistent, often sexually bemused Montalbano, moving with ease along zigzags created for him, teasing out threads of discrepancy that unravel the whole." —*Houston Chronicle*

"Sublime and darkly humorous . . . Camilleri balances his hero's personal and professional challenges perfectly and leaves the reader eager for more." —*Publishers Weekly* (starred review)

"The Montalbano mysteries offer *cose dolci* to the world-lit lover hankering for a whodunit." —*The Village Voice*

"In Sicily, where people do things as they please, Inspector Salvo Montalbano is a bona fide folk hero."
—*The New York Times Book Review*

"The books are full of sharp, precise characterizations and with subplots that make Montalbano endearingly human. . . . Like the antipasti that Montalbano contentedly consumes, the stories are light and easily consumed, leaving one eager for the next course."
—*New York Journal of Books*

"The reading of these little gems is fast and fun every step of the way." —*The New York Sun*

Also by Andrea Camilleri

Hunting Season

The Brewer of Preston

© Elvira Giorgianni

GAME OF MIRRORS

Andrea Camilleri, a bestseller in Italy and Germany, is the author of the popular Inspector Montalbano mystery series as well as historical novels that take place in nineteenth-century Sicily. His books have been made into Italian TV shows and translated into thirty-two languages. His thirteenth Montalbano novel, *The Potter's Field*, won the Crime Writers' Association International Dagger Award and was longlisted for the IMPAC Dublin Literary Award.

Stephen Sartarelli is an award-winning translator and the author of three books of poetry.

GAME OF MIRRORS

ANDREA CAMILLERI

Translated by Stephen Sartarelli

PENGUIN BOOKS

PENGUIN BOOKS

Published by the Penguin Group
Penguin Group (USA) LLC
375 Hudson Street
New York, New York 10014

USA | Canada | UK | Ireland | Australia
New Zealand | India | South Africa | China
penguin.com
A Penguin Random House Company

First published in Penguin Books 2015

Originally published in Italian as *Il gioco degli specchi* by Sellerio Editore, Palermo.

LIBRARY OF CONGRESS CATALOGING-IN-PUBLICATION DATA
Camilleri, Andrea.
[Il Gioco degli specchi. English]
Game of mirrors / Andrea Camilleri ; [translated by] Stephen Sartarelli.
pages cm
ISBN 978-0-14-312377-4 (pbk.)
1. Montalbano, Salvo (Fictitious character)—Fiction.
I. Sartarelli, Stephen, 1954—translator.   II. Title.
PQ4863.A3894G6813 2015
853'.914—dc23
2014032889

Printed in the United States of America
1 3 5 7 9 10 8 6 4 2

Set in Bembo
Designed by Jaye Zimet

GAME OF MIRRORS

1

He'd already been sitting for at least two hours, naked as the day God created him, in a chair that looked dangerously like an electric chair, wrists and ankles bound in iron bands to which were attached a great many wires that led into a metal cabinet all decorated on the outside with quadrants, pressure gauges, ampere meters, barometers, and little green, red, and blue lights blinking on and off without end. On his head was a sort of dome just like the hair dryers that hairdressers put on ladies' heads when giving them a perm, except that his was connected to the cabinet by a large black cable with hundreds of colored wires wound up inside.

The doctor, a man of about fifty with a helmet of hair parted in the middle, a goatee, gold-rimmed glasses, a smock that couldn't possibly have been any whiter, and an obnoxious, conceited air, had been asking him questions rapid-fire, such as:

1

"Who was Abraham Lincoln?"

"Who discovered America?"

"What do you think of when you see a woman with a nice backside?"

"What's nine times nine?"

"What would you rather eat, an ice-cream cone or a piece of moldy bread?"

"How many of Rome's seven kings were there?"

"What would you rather see, a funny movie or a fireworks display?"

"If a dog attacked, would you run away or stand your ground and growl?"

At a certain point the doctor suddenly fell silent, went *ahem ahem* with his throat, removed a stray thread from the sleeve of his smock, looked Montalbano in the eye, then sighed, shook his head in discouragement, sighed again, went *ahem ahem* again, pushed a button, and the iron bands around the inspector's wrists and ankles popped open and the dome rose up above his head.

"I guess the examination's over," the doctor said, going and sitting down behind the desk in a corner of the medical office. He started writing at the computer.

Montalbano stood up and grabbed his underpants and trousers in one hand, but he felt perplexed.

What was that *I guess* supposed to mean? Was the goddamned pain-in-the-ass examination over or not?

A week earlier he had received a memo signed by the

commissioner informing one and all that, in keeping with the new rules regarding personnel, issued personally in person by the minister of justice, he would have to undergo a mental health checkup at the Clinica Maria Vergine of Montelusa within ten days' time.

Why was it, he'd wondered at the time, that a minister can have the mental health of his subordinates checked, but a subordinate couldn't have the mental health of the minister checked? And so he'd protested to the commissioner.

"What do you want me to say, Montalbano? These are orders from on high. Your colleagues have all cooperated."

"Cooperate" was the watchword. If you didn't cooperate, rumors would fly that you were a pedophile, pimp, or serial nun rapist, and you would be forced to resign.

"Why don't you put your clothes back on?" the doctor asked.

"Why don't I . . . ?" the inspector muttered, searching for an explanation and beginning to get dressed. And that was when it happened. His trousers no longer fit. He was sure they were the same ones he'd had on when he came in, but they'd shrunk. Try as he might to suck in his gut, try as he might to squeeze himself into them, there was no way. They didn't fit. They were at least three sizes too small for him. In his last desperate attempt to put them on, he lost his balance, leaned one hand on a cart with a mysterious device on it, and the cart shot off like a rocket and crashed against the desk. The doctor leapt up in the air, startled.

"Have you gone mad?"

"My trousers . . . won't fit," the inspector stammered, trying to explain.

Getting up angrily, the doctor grabbed the trousers by the belt and pulled them up for him.

They fit perfectly.

Montalbano felt as ashamed as a little boy in kindergarten who needed the teacher's help in getting his clothes back on after going to the bathroom.

"I already had my doubts," the doctor said, sitting back down and resuming his writing at the keyboard, "but this last episode has swept away any lingering uncertainty."

What did he mean?

"Could you explain?"

"What's to explain? It's all so clear! I ask you what you think about if you see a beautiful woman's backside and you reply that you think of Abraham Lincoln!"

The inspector balked.

"I did? I said that?!"

"Do you want to contest the recording?"

Montalbano had a flash and suddenly understood. He'd been set up!

"It's a plot!" he started yelling. "You all want to make it look like I'm crazy!"

Before he'd even finished yelling, the door flew open and two burly orderlies burst in and seized him. Montalbano tried to break free, cursing and kicking in every direction, and then . . .

. . . and then he woke up. Bathed in sweat, with the sheet rolled around him so tightly that he couldn't move. Like a mummy.

When he finally managed to free himself, he looked at the clock. It was six in the morning.

The air coming in through the window was hot. Scirocco. The patch of sky he could see from his bed was entirely covered by a milky veil of cloud. He decided to lie there for another ten minutes.

No, the dream he'd just had was wrong. He would never go crazy, of that he was certain. If anything, he would start going senile little by little, forgetting the names and faces of the people dearest to him, until he sank into a sort of mindless solitude.

What nice, comforting thoughts he had first thing in the morning! His solution was to get up, race into the kitchen, and make coffee.

When he was ready to go out, he realized it was too early to go to the station. He opened the French door giving onto the veranda, sat down outside, and smoked a cigarette. It felt really hot. He decided it was better to go back inside and loll about the house until eight.

He got in his car and started driving down the little road that linked Marinella with the provincial road. About two hundred yards from his house was another small house, almost identical to his, which after sitting vacant for about two years was now inhabited by a childless couple, the Lombardos. The husband, Adriano, was a tall, stylish man of about forty-five who according to Fazio was the sole representative in all of Sicily of a large computer brand, a job that required him to travel a great deal. He owned a fast sports car. His wife, Liliana, about ten years younger than him, was an impressively attractive brunette from Turin. Tall with long, perfect legs, she must have engaged in some kind of sport. And when you saw her walking from behind, even if you were stark raving mad, you most certainly thought of Abraham Lincoln. For her part, she had a small Japanese car for driving around town.

Their relations with Montalbano went no further than "good morning" and "good afternoon," on those rare occasions when they crossed paths in their cars along the access road—which usually meant a complicated series of maneuvers, since the road was not wide enough for two vehicles to pass side by side.

That morning, out of the corner of his eye Montalbano saw Signora Lombardo's car just inside the open gate to her property, with the hood up and the lady bent over, looking inside. There seemed to be some sort of problem. Since he was in no hurry, almost without thinking he swerved to the right, went another ten yards or so, and pulled up in front of the open gate. Without getting out of the car, he asked:

"Need a hand?"

Signora Liliana beamed a grateful smile.

"It won't start!"

Montalbano got out but remained outside the gate.

"If you need to go into town, I can give you a lift."

"Thank you so much. I am in something of a rush, actually. But do you think you could have a quick look at the engine?"

"Believe me, signora, I don't know the first thing about cars."

"All right, then. I'll come with you."

She lowered the hood, came through the gate without shutting it, and got into the car through the door that Montalbano was holding open for her.

They drove off. Though the windows were all down, the car filled with her scent, which was at once delicate and penetrating.

"The problem is I don't know any mechanics, and my husband won't be back for another four days."

"You should give him a call."

Signora Lombardo seemed not to have heard the suggestion.

"Couldn't you recommend one yourself?"

"Of course. But I don't have his phone number on me. If you like, I can take you to his garage."

"Wonderful. You're so kind."

They didn't say anything else for the rest of the drive. Montalbano didn't want to seem nosy, and she, for her part, though polite and affable, clearly didn't want to get too familiar. After he introduced her to the mechanic, she turned and thanked him, and their brief encounter came to an end.

"Augello and Fazio here?"

"'Ey're onna scene, Chief."

"Send them to me."

"'Ow's 'ey gonna come, Chief?" Catarella asked, confused.

"What do you mean, how're they gonna come? On their legs, that's how!"

"But 'ey ain't 'ere, Chief, 'ey're onna scene where the scene is."

"And where's this scene?"

"Wait an' I'll have a look."

He picked up a piece of paper and read it.

"'Ere i'ssez Via Pissaviacane, nummer twinny-eight."

"Are you sure it's called Via Pissaviacane?"

"Sure as death, Chief."

He'd never heard of it.

"Ring Fazio and put him through to my office."

The telephone rang.

"Fazio, what's going on?"

"Somebody put a bomb in front of a warehouse in Via Pisacane very early this morning. No injuries, just a terrible fright and some broken windows. And a big hole in the metal shutter, naturally."

"What's inside the warehouse?"

"Nothing, actually. It's been empty for almost a year."

"I see. And the owner?"

"I questioned him. I'll tell you everything later. We'll be back in about an hour, max."

He started grudgingly signing some papers, just so that the huge stack on his desk might find a slightly less precarious equilibrium. For some time now Montalbano had formed a clear idea about a mysterious phenomenon, but he preferred not discussing it with anyone. Because if he did, they certainly would consider him mad. The phenomenon was the following: How was it that the number of documents actually managed to increase during the night? How could one explain that when he left in the evening, the stack was three feet high, and when he returned in the morning it was three and a quarter, long before the day's mail was delivered? There could be only one explanation. When the office was dark and deserted, the documents, unseen by anyone, would scatter around the room, shucking off their slipcovers, folders, and binders, and indulge in unbridled orgies, interminable copulations, unspeakable cluster fucks. So that the following morning, the fruits born of their nights of sin would increase the volume and height of the stack.

The telephone rang.

"Chief, 'at'd be Francischino onna line, wantin' a talk t'yiz poissonally in poisson."

Who on earth was that? But rather than waste time with Catarella, he had him put the call through.

"Who is this?"

"It's Francischino, Inspector, the mechanic."

"Ah, right. What is it?"

"I'm calling you from the Lombardos' home. Somebody busted up their engine. What should I do? Tow it into the garage, or leave it here?"

"I'm sorry, but why are you asking me?"

"Because the lady don't answer her cell phone, and since she's your friend—"

"She's not my friend, Francischì, she's just an acquaintance. I don't know what to tell you."

"All right, sorry."

One of the things the mechanic said stuck in the inspector's mind.

"Why do you say somebody 'busted up' her engine?"

"Because that's what happened. They opened the hood and did a load of damage."

"Are you saying it was done on purpose?"

"I know my trade, Inspector."

So who could have anything against the lovely Liliana Lombardo?

"So what's this all about?" the inspector asked Fazio and Augello as soon as they sat down in front of him.

It was up to Deputy Inspector Domenico Augello, whom everyone called Mimì, to answer. And, in fact, he said:

"In my opinion, it's a case of nonpayment of protection money. But Fazio doesn't agree."

"Let's hear you out first," said Montalbano.

"The warehouse belongs to a certain Angelino Arnone, who also owns a grocery, a bakery, and a shoe store. That makes three protection-racket payments he has to pay. Either he forgot to pay a couple, or they upped the price and he refused. And so, to bring him back in line, they sent him a warning. That's what I think."

"And what's this Arnone have to say?"

"The usual bullshit we've heard a thousand times before. That he's never paid the racket because he's never been asked to pay, that he has no enemies and is loved by all."

"And what do you think?" Montalbano asked Fazio.

"I dunno, Chief, the whole thing just doesn't add up to me."

"Why not?"

"Because it would be the first time they set a bomb off in front of a warehouse to get somebody to pay the racket. What did they damage? His metal shutter? With a few euros it's all taken care of. Whereas according to normal procedure, they should have put it in front of his grocery or bakery or shoe store. In that case the warning would make sense."

The inspector didn't know what to say. On the other hand, Fazio's doubt wasn't really so far-fetched.

"So why, in your opinion, didn't they stick to normal procedure this time?"

"I have no answer, to be honest. But if you'll allow me, I'd like to know more about this Angelino Arnone."

"Fine, gather your information and then let me know. Oh, and just what kind of bomb was it?"

"A classic time bomb. Inside a cardboard box that looked like it was left there for the garbage collectors."

On his way to Enzo's trattoria for lunch, the inspector happened to read the name of a short, narrow street he went up and down at least twice a day: Via Pisacane.

He'd never noticed the name before. He slowed down in front of number 28. Arnone's warehouse, the ground floor of a three-story building, was wedged between a hardware store and the door leading to the apartments above. The bomb had been placed not in the middle of the metal shutter, but on the far right.

At Enzo's he gorged himself. A variety of antipasti, spaghetti in squid ink, a sampling of pasta in clam sauce, and a main course of striped surmullet (actually two generous helpings).

So a walk along the jetty to the flat rock under the lighthouse became a necessity, despite the heat.

He spent an hour there, smoking and pestering a crab, then headed back to the office.

He parked and got out of the car, but to enter the building he had to push aside with his foot a large package blocking the entrance.

Something like a flash went off in his brain.

"Cat, what's that parcel in the doorway?"

"Sorry, Chief, but summon from a'ministration's comin' straightaways ta pick it up. Eight packitches o' forms, quessionaires, an' litterhead arrived."

How was it that the Ministry of Justice had the money to increase the bureaucratic pains in the ass but didn't have any to buy gas for the mobile units?

"Is Fazio in?"

"Yessir."

"Send 'im to me."

Fazio arrived with an excuse.

"Chief, I haven't had a free minute all morning to look into Arnone."

"Have a seat; I want to tell you something. Today I discovered, entirely by chance, that one of the streets I usually take to go to lunch was Via Pisacane. So I had a look."

Fazio looked at him inquisitively.

"Judging from the marks left by the blast and the hole it made in the shutter, it looked to me like the bomb was placed at the far right end of the shutter. Is that right?"

"Yes."

"In other words, close to number twenty-six, which is the entrance to the rest of the building. Right?"

"Right."

"Okay, now listen up. I have a theory. If a tenant coming out or going into the building first thing in the morning sees a cardboard box blocking the doorway, what does he do?"

"Probably pushes it aside with his foot," said Fazio. Then, a moment later: "Holy shit!"

"Exactly. It's possible the bomb was not a warning for Arnone, but for someone who lives in that building."

"You're right. Which complicates things and means we have a lot more work to do."

"Do you want me to talk to Inspector Augello about it?" Fazio grimaced.

"If I could bring Gallo along . . ." he said.

"Sure, go ahead," said the inspector.

Augello came in about half an hour later.

"Have you got a minute?"

"I've got as much time as you need, Mimì."

"I've been thinking about what Fazio said this morning about the bomb. And it is indeed an anomaly. So I asked myself why the bomb was placed at the far right end of the shutter and not in the middle. Because right beside the warehouse is the entrance to a three-story apartment building. So my question is: Couldn't the bomb have been intended for that building? And a tenant just pushed it aside without realizing that it had a bomb inside?"

Montalbano gave him a look of jubilation.

"Do you know that's a brilliant observation, Mimì? Congratulations. I'll tell Fazio to start investigating the building's tenants right away."

Augello stood up and went back to his office feeling satisfied.

Why disappoint him? Young Eagle Scout Salvo Montalbano had done his good deed for the day.

2

When passing by the Lombardos' house on his way home, he immediately noticed that her car was no longer there, and through an open window in the back he could see a bedroom all lit up and Signora Lombardo standing in front of an open armoire.

The moment he set foot in his house, he froze, unable to move, beset by a sudden doubt. How should he proceed with his lovely neighbor? Francischino surely must have told her that someone had damaged her engine on purpose. So was it or was it not his duty, as a police inspector, to offer to help her find who had done it and to protect her from further danger? Perhaps the lady was expecting him to offer to intervene. Or should he just sit tight and say nothing, since she hadn't reported anything yet?

But what if the lady hadn't yet had the time to report it?

As he was searching for the right answer, another doubt assailed him, this one of a strictly personal nature. If Signora Liliana was not a beautiful woman but a cross-eyed, toothless, bowlegged crone, would he still be so interested in her?

Feeling offended for having had such a thought, he answered himself sincerely: yes, he would be just as interested in her.

And this was enough to persuade him to stop wasting time and go ring the bell at the Lombardos' gate.

He walked there, given how close their house was to his.

Signora Liliana seemed quite pleased to see him. It was said that the Piedmontese were false and polite, but her welcome didn't seem the least bit false.

"Come in, come in! Just follow me."

She was wearing a little dress as light as could be, short and formfitting. It looked as if it were painted on her skin. Montalbano followed her like an automaton, totally hypnotized by the harmonious undulations of the spheres moving before him. Two more spheres to be added to the celestial one of which the poets sang.

"Shall we go out on the veranda?"

"With pleasure."

The veranda was exactly the same as his, except for the table and chairs, which were fancier and more modern.

"Can I get you something?"

"No, thanks, no need to bother."

"I should tell you, Inspector, I've got some excellent vodka. But if you haven't eaten dinner yet . . ."

"Actually, something cold might be nice in this heat, thank you."

"I'll go and get you some."

She returned with a bottle of vodka in a bucket of ice, two small stemmed glasses, and an ashtray.

"I'll have just a little drop to keep you company," she said. "If you feel like smoking—"

They heard a cell phone ring inside the house.

"Damn, what a pain! Excuse me for a second. In the meantime please help yourself."

She went inside and must have gone into the bedroom to talk, perhaps closing the door, because the inspector couldn't hear even the faintest murmur.

The phone call was long enough for Montalbano to smoke a whole cigarette.

When she returned, Signora Liliana's face was quite red and she was breathing heavily. And her panting, incidentally, had an additionally lovely result, evoking other celestial spheres, since she clearly wasn't wearing a bra. She must have just had a rather animated exchange.

"I'm sorry, that was Adriano, my husband. An unexpected hassle. But you haven't had anything to drink! Here, let me serve you."

She poured two fingers' worth of vodka into one of the little glasses, which she held out for Montalbano, then gave herself a rather hefty dose in her own, which she brought to her lips and downed in a single draft.

So much for the "little drop"!

"To what do I owe the pleasure of your visit, Inspector?"

"I don't know whether the mechanic told you . . ."

"That it's going to take a long time to fix the engine? Yes, he did, and in fact I had him tow the car to his garage. It's not going to be easy for me to go back and forth to Montelusa. It's true there's the bus, but its schedule is so odd . . ."

"I usually leave for the office around eight in the morning. If you want I can give you a ride, at least on the way in . . ."

"Thanks, I think I'll take you up on that. I'll be ready and waiting tomorrow at eight."

Montalbano returned to the subject that interested him.

"Did the mechanic tell you how the engine got damaged?"

She laughed. *Matre santa*, what a laugh! It hit him right in the gut. She sounded like a dove in love.

"There was no need for me to ask him. I'm a terrible driver; I must have subjected that poor engine—"

"No, that's not it."

"It's not?"

"No. Your car's engine was intentionally damaged, quite on purpose."

She immediately turned pale. Montalbano continued:

"That's the mechanic's opinion, and he knows what he's talking about."

Liliana poured herself more vodka and drank it. She started looking out at the sea without saying anything.

"Did you use your car yesterday, signora?"

"Yes. I was out until evening, and up to then it ran just fine."

"So it happened last night. Someone must have climbed your gate, raised the hood, and rendered the engine unusable. Did you hear any noise?"

"Nothing at all."

"And yet the car was parked very close to the bedroom window."

"I said I didn't hear anything!"

Montalbano pretended not to notice that she'd answered crossly. But having come this far, he might as well go all the way.

"Do you have any idea who it might have been?"

"No."

But as soon as she'd said no, Liliana seemed to change her mind.

She turned and looked Montalbano in the eye.

"You know, Inspector, I'm often alone, and for long periods of time. And so I'm an attractive target for . . . In short, I've had some trouble. Just imagine, one night some idiot came and knocked on the shutter to my bedroom window! So this might have been done by someone wanting to avenge himself for my indifference . . ."

"Have you had any explicit propositions?"

"As many as you like."

"Could you give me the names of any of these, er, suitors of yours?"

"But can't you see I don't even know what they look like? They call me up and tell me their names, but it might just be made up, and then they're off on a string of obscenities."

Montalbano pulled a piece of paper out of his pocket and wrote something on it.

"Here's my home phone number. Don't hesitate to call me if anyone comes by and bothers you during the night."

Then he stood up and said good-bye. Liliana walked him out to the gate.

"I'm so grateful you're taking an interest in this. See you tomorrow."

After scarfing down a dish of *pasta 'ncasciata* and a huge serving of eggplant parmesan, both prepared by his housekeeper Adelina, he went outside and sat down on the veranda.

The sky was so full of stars it looked as if you could reach up and touch them with your hand. The gentle wind that had risen felt like a caress on his skin. After five minutes of this, however, Montalbano realized it wouldn't work. He absolutely needed a long walk along the beach for digestive purposes.

He went down to the beach, but instead of turning right in the direction of Scala dei Turchi, as he always did, he turned left, towards town. And thus he passed directly in front of the Lombardos' house.

But he hadn't done it on purpose. Or had he?

All the lights were off, and he couldn't tell whether the French door to the veranda was open or closed. Perhaps Liliana had eaten, knocked back a few more little glasses of vodka, and gone to bed.

At that moment, along the main road, a car made a U-turn and its headlights briefly lit up the rear of the house.

That was enough for Montalbano to see distinctly that there was a car stopped outside the gate.

He got worried. Want to bet the unknown engine basher had come back to do more damage? And that Liliana had phoned him to ask for help, and he hadn't been there to take the call because he was out walking on the beach?

He changed course and headed for the Lombardos' house. When he got to the veranda he saw that the French door was closed from the inside. And so he circled very carefully around the house to the back.

The car, a green Volvo with the license plate XZ 452 BG, was parked with its nose up against the closed gate. Through the carefully closed shutters of what Montalbano knew to be the bedroom, a thin shaft of light filtered out. The window was low enough that a person's head came up to the sill.

He went up to it and immediately heard Liliana moaning. Certainly not in pain.

Montalbano rushed away. And to work off the agitation that had suddenly come over him, he resumed his walk along the beach.

That his lovely, amiable neighbor was telling him a pack of lies had dawned on Montalbano even during his visit. And what was happening at that very moment in the signora's bedroom was the irrefutable confirmation of this.

At this point he would have bet the house that the person who'd phoned her was not her husband but another man.

Probably the brilliant idea of vandalizing her car's engine had come to a lover of hers whom she'd grown tired of and given his walking papers to make room for the owner of the Volvo. Or else she'd had a quarrel with the owner of the Volvo, who'd then lost his head and taken it out on her car. Then there'd been the reconciliation, of which he'd just heard part of the soundtrack.

Therefore Liliana knew perfectly well not only the first and last names and addresses of the men who called her up, but also their vital statistics and distinguishing features.

At this point Montalbano concluded that the whole affair was a private matter between Liliana and her lovers and decided that there was no more reason for him to get involved.

And so, after his customary good-night phone call to Livia, with the requisite beginnings of a squabble, he went to bed.

The following morning at eight o'clock sharp, Liliana was waiting for him in the driveway. Naturally the Volvo was no longer parked in front of the gate or anywhere in the vicinity. Perhaps because it was even hotter than the day before, she was wearing a dress similar to the one she'd had on the previous night, except this one was light blue. And it had the same devastating effect.

She was fresh and well rested. And well scented.

"Everything okay?" the inspector asked.

He'd managed to ask the question without insinuation.

"I slept like a baby," Liliana said, smiling like a cat that had just eaten a can of its favorite food and was licking its chops.

I don't think babies sleep the way you do, Montalbano thought to himself.

At that exact moment a car coming the other way decided to pass a truck at high speed.

Collision would have been inevitable had Montalbano not swerved sharply to the right with a swiftness of reflex that surprised him more than anyone, taking advantage of a wide shoulder and getting quickly back onto the road. At once he felt the weight of Liliana's body leaning against his, and a second later the woman's inert head fell onto his legs.

She'd fainted.

Montalbano froze. He'd never been in so awkward a situation in his life.

What was he to do?

Cursing the saints, he saw a filling station just ahead with a café-bar in back.

He pulled up, laid Liliana down on the seat a little better, dashed into the bar, bought a bottle of mineral water, and returned. Sitting back down in the car, he wet his handkerchief with the water, took her in his arms, and began to daub her face with the cold water. Moments later she opened her eyes and, remembering the danger they'd been in, she cried out and held him tight, her cheek up against his.

"Come on, there's a good girl. It's over now."

He could feel her trembling. When he started gently stroking her back, she held him even tighter.

Luckily there were no other cars around, or he would have felt embarrassed at what their occupants might be thinking.

"Here, drink some water."

She obeyed. Then Montalbano drank some himself.

"You're all sweaty," she said. "Were you scared, too?"

"Yes."

A big lie. He hadn't had time to get scared. If he was sweating and thirsty it was for a reason he couldn't reveal to her, since she was the cause.

The inspector was also angry with himself for the simple fact that holding a beautiful woman in his arms had put him in a state of agitation worse than a teenager's in a similar situation. As if it were the first time. So perhaps aging was a kind of regression back into youth? No, what the hell? If anything it was a progression towards imbecility.

After about ten minutes, they were fit to head off again.

"Where shall I drop you off?"

"You can leave me at the bus stop for Montelusa. I'm terribly late now."

When it came time to say good-bye, Liliana held his hand and squeezed it.

"Listen," she said. "You've been so kind to me . . . Could I invite you to dinner at my place tonight?"

Was it perhaps her night off from the guy with the Volvo? But the real question—and a crucial one at that—was: If the lady didn't know how to cook, what sort of ghastly slop would he be forced to ingest?

Liliana seemed to read his mind.

"Don't worry, I'm a decent cook," she said.

"I'd be happy to come, thanks."

———

"Listen, Cat," said the inspector, going into the switchboard operator's closet. "Get Francischino's garage on the line and put it through to my office, would you?"

"Straightaways, Chief. Jeezis, 'ass some fancy perfume ya got on today!"

Montalbano gawked.

"Me?!"

Catarella brought his nose up to the inspector's jacket.

"Yeah, 'iss you awright."

It must have been Liliana's perfume.

He headed for his office, muttering curses, then picked up the ringing phone.

"Tell me something, Francischì. Did you tell Signora Lombardo that her car's engine was intentionally damaged?"

"Yessir."

"And do you think they made a lot of noise when damaging it that way?"

"Absolutely, Inspector! They musta made one hell of a racket! Or else how would they a done it? They even used a hammer!"

And therefore during the destruction of her car's engine Liliana was either holed up inside her house in terror or . . . Yes, that was the more likely scenario. She could well have spent part of the night away, with the man with the Volvo, and when she returned in the morning she found the nice little present her former lover had left her . . .

"May I?" said Fazio, poking his head inside the door.

"Come in and sit down. Any news?"

Fazio sniffed the air. "What's that scent?"

Jeez, what a pain!

"You can plug your nose if you don't want to smell it," Montalbano said gruffly.

Fazio realized he should let it drop.

"Chief, you know who lives in that apartment building in Via Pisacane? Two ex-cons and Carlo Nicotra."

Montalbano gave him a confused look.

"You mention Nicotra as if he's the pope or something. Who is the guy?"

"Carlo Nicotra got married to a niece of old man Sinagra six years ago and apparently the family gave him the job of overseeing all the drug dealers on the island."

"A kind of inspector general?"

"Exactly."

All at once the inspector remembered. Why hadn't it occurred to him sooner? Apparently, he thought bitterly, his age was starting to play nasty jokes on him.

"But isn't he the guy who was shot three years ago?"

"He certainly is. Right in the chest. An inch and a half to the left and it would have burst his heart."

"Wait . . . wait . . . And isn't he the same guy whose car was blown up last year?"

"The very same."

"So this bomb in Via Pisacane would seem to have had a precise address, wouldn't it?"

"So it would seem."

"But you're not convinced."

"Nope."

"Me neither. Tell me why."

"Well, first they shot Nicotra, then he was supposed to have been blown up with his car the moment he turned the key in the ignition, except that he'd sent his assistant to go and get his car, and the guy got killed in the process . . . What I mean is that Carlo Nicotra is not the kind of man they send warnings to. They just try to kill him, period."

"I totally agree. At any rate, I'd still keep an eye on him. And who are the two ex-cons?"

Fazio thrust a hand in his pocket and pulled out a sheet of paper. Montalbano frowned.

"If you start reciting the names of the father and mother and the date and place of birth of these convicts, I'm going to make you eat that piece of paper."

Fazio turned red and said nothing.

"You would have been happier working as a clerk at the records office for a living," said the inspector.

Fazio began putting the piece of paper slowly back in his pocket. He was acting like a man dying of thirst who had just been refused a glass of water. Young Eagle Scout Salvo Montalbano decided to do his good deed for the day.

"Oh, okay, go ahead and read it."

Fazio's face lit up like a lightbulb. He unfolded the piece of paper and held it in front of him.

"The first one is Vincenzo Giannino, son of Giuseppe Giannino and Michela Tabita, born in Barrafranca on March 7, 1970. He's done a total of ten years in prison for armed robbery, breaking and entering, and assaulting a public official. The second one is Stefano Tallarita, son of Salvatore Tallarita and Giovanna Tosto, born in Vigàta on August 22, 1958. He's currently in Montelusa Prison, serving a term for narcotics trafficking. He'd already been in once for four years, also for dealing."

He folded up the paper and put it back in his pocket.

3

"Excuse me," said Montalbano, "but if Tallarita's in jail, who's living at his place in Via Pisacane?"

Fazio again pulled the piece of paper out of his pocket. He looked at his boss as though asking permission to read. The inspector shrugged and threw his hands up. With a beatific expression on his face, Fazio, now in seventh heaven, began to read.

"Wife Francesca, née Calcedonio, forty-five years old, born in Montereale; son Arturo, twenty-three years old, and daughter Stella, twenty years old."

"What does Arturo do?"

"I know he works in Montelusa. I think he's a salesman in a clothing store for men and women."

"And the daughter?"

"A student at the University of Palermo."

"Do they seem like bomb targets to you?"

"No, sir."

"So it was intended for either Arnone or, despite our opinions, Nicotra."

"What should I do?"

"Keep working on those two."

Fazio made as if to leave, but the inspector stopped him with a gesture. Fazio sat back down and waited for Montalbano to ask him something, but his boss remained silent. The fact was that the inspector didn't know where to begin. Then he made up his mind.

"Do you remember when you asked me about my neighbors a little while ago?"

"The Lombardos? Yes."

What a superb cop's memory Fazio had!

"Do you know the husband?"

"The first time I saw him was when he came in to the station to report the theft of a suitcase he'd left on the backseat of his car."

"Did the thieves force the door open?"

"Yeah."

"What was in the suitcase?"

"Personal effects, according to him. He was heading out on a tour of the island. I believe he's the representative of a computer company. And truth be told, he didn't seem that keen on reporting the crime."

Then it must be some kind of family vice, this not wanting to file reports.

"Explain."

"Before leaving Vigàta, he'd stopped at the Bar Castiglione for a cup of coffee. And while he was inside, some guy on a motorcycle smashed the car window, opened the door, and grabbed the suitcase. A municipal patrolman then showed up, and it was this cop who made Lombardo file a report; otherwise the guy would have taken off without doing anything, not even about his broken car window."

"And have you ever seen his wife?"

"Just once. And I certainly haven't forgotten her."

Montalbano knew what he meant. And so he decided to tell him the whole story, from the moment he first saw Liliana looking under her car's hood to the previous night and the ride he'd given her this morning.

"So what do you think?" he asked in conclusion.

"Chief, it could be revenge on the part of a jilted lover, as you say, or it could be just about anything else. With a woman like that, anything is possible. And it's clear she knows who did it but has no intention whatsoever of reporting him."

He did not ask why Montalbano had become interested in the matter in the first place. But he had a puzzled look on his face.

"What's wrong?"

"I'm sorry, Chief, but there's something that doesn't . . ."

He trailed off, seeming confused.

"Are you going to tell me what's wrong or not?"

"What time do you think it was when you heard Signora Lombardo making love?"

Montalbano thought about this for a minute.

"Definitely between eleven and a quarter past. Why?"

"I'm sure I'm mistaken," said Fazio.

"Well, tell me just the same."

"Remember how I just now said 'the first time I saw Lombardo'? I said the 'first time' because there was a second time, too."

"And when was that?"

"Yesterday evening we went to dinner at my sister-in-law's place at eight, and we left at ten thirty. Since we live nearby, we walked. Well, on our way back, there was a drunk in the middle of the road, and a car had to slow down. It was a big sports car, and at the wheel was none other than Lombardo, or so I thought."

"What direction was he going in?"

"Toward Marinella."

"Are you sure the car wasn't a green Volvo?"

"Come on, Chief, is that some kind of joke?"

"But do you realize what you're saying? No, it's simply not possible that—"

"Exactly. It was probably a mistake," Fazio cut him off.

"Chief, 'at'd be yer 'ousekipper Adilina onna line."

"Put her on. What is it, Adelì?"

"Isspector, I gonna meck *arancini* tonite, an' I wannata ask ya if ya do me the 'onor a comin' a eat atta my place a tonite."

Montalbano felt a rush of happiness and unhappiness at once. Savoring Adelina's arancini rice balls was a total experience, a pinnacle of existence. Once you'd tasted them, they remained forever etched in your memory like some sort of paradise lost. For this reason, the offer to return to the Garden of Eden for one evening was not something to be lightly dismissed.

The inspector, however, had committed himself to going to Liliana's for dinner and didn't feel like canceling. He couldn't even if he wanted to, since he didn't have her cell phone number.

"Adelì, thank you so much, but I can't come."

"An' why not? My boy Pasquali's gonna come wit' 'is wife anna my granson, Salvuzzo, cuz iss 'is birthday."

Montalbano was the godfather of Pasquale's son, having held the child at his baptism.

"Adelì, I can't come because I've already been invited to dinner by my neighbor, the young woman who lives in the little house nearby . . ."

"I know her! I talk a to her! Whatta goo'-lookin' lady she is! Anna she's nice anna polite too! Is 'er husban' there too?"

"No, he's away on business."

"Then you bring 'er here! I tell ya f'ya own good! My arancini mecka miracles!" And she started laughing insinuatingly.

Adelina couldn't stand Livia, and the feeling was mutual. Whenever Livia came to stay with Montalbano for a few days, Adelina would disappear until the inspector was alone again. Therefore she would be delighted if he was unfaithful to her.

"I don't know how to reach her."

"Don' mecka me laugh! Isspector Montalbano donna know how to fine a woman!"

And indeed, at that moment he knew what to do.

"Listen, I'll call you back in ten minutes."

He called up Francischino's garage, asked him for Liliana's number, then rang her.

"Montalbano here."

"Don't tell me you can't come tonight!"

He told her about Adelina's invitation.

"They're rather simple people," he added.

He neglected to tell her that Pasquale was a habitual offender and that he'd had to send him to jail himself two or three times.

"All right. But are her arancini like the ones they serve on the ferryboat?"

Montalbano became indignant.

"That's blasphemy," he said.

She laughed.

"What time will you come to pick me up?"

"How's eight thirty sound?"

"Sounds good, but my invitation still stands."

"I don't understand."

"You still owe me a dinner at my house."

He called Adelina back and told her he'd be bringing Signora Lombardo.

His housekeeper was pleased.

⬛

At Enzo's, with the evening's arancini to look forward to, the inspector ate lightly, skipping the antipasto and eating only one serving of the main course.

But he took a stroll along the jetty anyway, not for digestive but for meditative purposes.

He was feeling troubled by what Fazio had told him— that is, that he'd seen Liliana's husband in Vigàta while she was in bed with her lover.

True, Fazio had admitted that he might be mistaken, but he'd reached this conclusion by way of logic. Because if Lombardo had been in Vigàta, things could not have gone as smoothly as they had. Fazio's first, instinctual reaction as a policeman, however, was to recognize Lombardo inside his sports car. And Montalbano had a lot of faith in Fazio's instincts. He therefore had to take into consideration, at least theoretically, the hypothesis that Lombardo was returning home to Marinella that evening, after being away for a few days.

Then how to explain that he hadn't caught Liliana with another man? Had he purposely avoided doing so?

First answer: Lombardo wasn't going home, but to Montereale or Fiacca or Trapani or only he knew where, and in a hurry, and therefore hadn't planned to stop at home, not even for a moment, to say hello to his wife.

But this answer didn't make sense, because going in that direction he would have had no choice but to pass by his house, and he couldn't have failed to notice the Volvo parked outside the gate. At the very least, he should have been curious enough to stop.

Second answer: Lombardo was in fact going home, but saw the Volvo, concluded that Liliana had company, and so drove past unseen. In this case, it was possible that he and his wife had an open marriage in which each did whatever he or she felt like doing.

But the second answer didn't make sense either. Because in that case he could very easily have waited nearby for Liliana's encounter to be over, and then gone home. Whereas there was no trace whatsoever of him when Liliana was waiting to be picked up the following morning.

Third answer: Lombardo called his wife to let her know that he would be stopping by in the evening, since he had to pass that way. And the call came in when he, Montalbano, was in their house. Liliana tells him he can't come by because she's busy. And they have an argument. But in the end the husband does what his wife asks.

Unavoidable conclusion: Lombardo in any case didn't care how his wife behaved.

But all this was predicated on the assumption that Fazio had not been mistaken in recognizing Lombardo.

"Ahh Chief, 'ere'd be summon 'at calls 'isself Arrigone 'oo amoijently wants a talk t'yiz poissonally in poisson."

"On the phone or the premises?"

"Onna premisses."

"Did he say what he wanted?"

"Nah, Chief."

"All right, show him in."

Catarella appeared in the doorway and then stood aside, saying:

"Signor Arrigone."

"Arnone, Angelino Arnone," the man said, correcting him and coming in.

He was a short bald man of about sixty, and, despite the designer suit he was wearing and a pair of shoes that must have cost him a king's ransom, it was immediately obvious that he was of peasant origins.

"Wait," the inspector said to Catarella, and then, turning to Arnone: "If I remember correctly, you, sir, would be the owner of the warehouse that—"

"Precisely."

"Catarella, have Fazio and Inspector Augello come to my office."

"Straightaways, Chief."

"You can sit down in the meanwhile, Mr. Arnone."

The man sat down on the edge of a chair. He must have been nervous, because he mopped his sweaty brow with his handkerchief. Or maybe he was just suffering from the heat.

Augello and Fazio came in.

"You already know one another, correct?" the inspector asked.

"Yes, yes," the three said in unison.

When they had all sat down, Montalbano looked inquisitively at Arnone. Who, before answering the inspector's unspoken question, passed his handkerchief over his face and neck. No, he wasn't hot; he was extremely nervous.

"I . . . I didn't think the bomb . . . I just . . . I didn't think it had anything to do with me. And that's what I told these gentlemen."

"Would you repeat it for me?" Montalbano asked.

"Repeat what for you?"

"The reason why you were convinced the bomb had nothing to do with you."

"Well . . ." Arnone began.

And then he stopped.

"'Well' isn't quite enough for me," said the inspector.

"Well . . . first of all, I don't have any enemies."

"Signor Arnone, considering that all you're doing is insulting me, I would ask you please to leave this room at once."

Arnone started sweating rivers. His handkerchief by now was completely soaked.

"I . . . insulting you, sir?"

"You were indirectly treating me like an idiot by expecting me to believe that you have no enemies. So either you start telling us clearly why you came here, or you leave."

"I got an anonymous letter."

"When?"

"With the last mail delivery."

"Have you got it with you?"

"Yessir."

"Give it to me."

Arnone stuck his hand in his jacket pocket, pulled out an envelope, and set it down on the desk.

Montalbano didn't touch it.

"How many lines?"

Arnone looked at sea. He glanced at Fazio, then Augello, then looked back at the inspector.

"I don't understand."

"I'm simply asking if you remember how many lines there were in the letter. Fazio, have you got anything to give the gentleman for his sweat?"

Fazio handed him a Kleenex.

"I don't remember."

"But did you read the letter?"

"Of course."

"How many times?"

"Uhh . . . I dunno, four, five times."

"And you don't remember how many lines there were? Strange."

Montalbano finally picked up the envelope.

The address was written in block letters:

ANGELINO ARNONE
VIA ALLORO 122
VIGÀTA

He pulled out the folded half page that was inside and handed the envelope to Augello.

This is to tell you the bomb was intended for your warehouse, and you know why

"Barely a line and a half, Signor Arnone," Montalbano commented.

Arnone said nothing.

"Do you believe it?" the inspector asked.

"Believe what?"

"The anonymous letter."

"They sent it to me, no . . . ?"

"You change your mind too easily, if I may say so. First you think the bomb wasn't intended for your warehouse, and then, after receiving an anonymous letter . . ."

Arnone shook his head in distress.

"You get me all confused if you do that," the inspector continued. "Never mind. So you now admit that the bomb was intended for your warehouse?"

"Yes, sir, I do."

"It's not like if they send you another anonymous letter saying the opposite you'll change your mind, is it?"

Arnone was flummoxed. He shook his head "no."

"What do you want from us, Signor Arnone? Protection?"

"I just came . . . to tell you . . . I made a mistake . . . Tha'ss all."

"So you admit you have some enemies?"

Arnone threw his hands up.

"Please answer me verbally."

"Yes."

"So why, if you have enemies, don't you want to ask us for protection?"

Fazio started feeling sorry for Arnone and handed him another tissue.

"W . . . ell . . . if ya wanna . . . gimme . . . this protection . . ."

"Then you'll have to work with us."

"Wha'? How?"

"By giving us the name of someone you think is your enemy."

The color of Arnone's face was now verging on green.

"But that means . . . I have to think about it a little."

"I understand perfectly, sir. Think about it at your leisure, and then get in touch with Inspector Augello when you're ready."

Montalbano stood up, and they all stood up.

"I thank you for doing your duty as a citizen. Have a good day. Fazio, please see the gentleman out."

"I don't understand why you treated him that way!" Augello exclaimed after the others had left.

"Mimì, I think your engine is starting to misfire," said Montalbano.

Fazio returned.

"What sons of bitches!" he said, sitting down.

He'd understood everything, like Montalbano.

"And who would these sons of bitches happen to be?" Augello asked.

"Mimì," said the inspector, "since you, from the very start, got it into your head to believe that the bomb was intended for Arnone, you saw the anonymous letter as confirmation of that."

"And is that somehow not the case?"

"No, it's not. The letter would have us believe that's the case, but neither Fazio nor I am convinced of it."

"And why not?"

"If the letter had been genuine, do you really think Arnone would have let us see it?"

Augello didn't answer. He looked doubtful.

"No, he certainly would not have brought it to us," the inspector continued. "And if he did, it's because he was forced to do so."

"By whom?"

"By those who planted the bomb, who are probably the same people he pays protection money to. They probably called him up, told him they were sending him an anonymous letter, and ordered him to show it to us. And Arnone did as he was told."

"So the bomb was intended for number twenty-six, not for twenty-eight," Augello said, as if now convinced.

"Exactly. Anyway, have you forgotten that you made the same hypothesis yourself?"

Fazio looked at Montalbano but said nothing.

"And Fazio, in fact, is investigating the tenants in number twenty-six," Montalbano concluded.

For the moment they had nothing more to say to each other.

Five minutes later, the inspector left the office. It had occurred to him that he should buy a present for Salvuzzo, his godson.

4

When he got home at seven thirty, he dashed into the shower, changed clothes, and was all ready when the doorbell rang at eight thirty.

He went to open the door, and there was Liliana. She wasn't wearing one of her man-killing dresses, but slacks, blouse, and jacket.

"You're early," said Montalbano.

"I know. I decided to take advantage of the situation."

"What do you mean?"

"I wanted to see your house."

She started looking around respectfully, stopping in front of the paintings and the bookcase.

"It certainly doesn't seem like the home of a police inspector. And our house has one more room."

"Why doesn't it seem like the home of a police inspector?"

She smiled enchantingly, looked him in the eye, and didn't answer. Then went out and sat down on the veranda.

"I don't have any aperitifs to offer you," said Montalbano. "But I've got a nice, light white wine in the fridge . . ."

"Some light white wine sounds good."

The inspector poured himself a finger's worth, since he had to drive, but filled her glass up three-quarters of the way.

"I found out you have a girlfriend," Liliana said out of the blue, gazing at the sea as she said it.

"Who told you?"

She smiled.

"I asked around. Feminine curiosity. How long have you been together?"

"Forever."

"What's her name?"

"Livia. She lives in Genoa."

"Does she come to see you often?"

"Not as often as I'd like."

"Poor thing."

The comment made Montalbano bristle. He didn't like to talk about his own private matters, and he didn't like other people taking pity on him. On top of that, he thought he heard a note of irony in her voice. Was she making fun of him because he was forced to remain celibate for long periods of time? He looked at his watch visibly, so she would see. But Liliana continued to drink slowly.

Then, all at once, in a single, brusque motion, as though suddenly in a hurry, she gulped down the rest of her wine and stood up.

"We can go now."

When they were in the car, she said:

"I don't want to stay late. Afterwards I'd like to have a little time with you. I need to talk to you."

"You could save some time and start now."

"No, not in the car."

"Tell me what it's about, at least."

"No. I'm sorry, but it's sort of an unpleasant subject, and I don't want to spoil my appetite."

He didn't insist.

Before going to Adelina's house, the inspector pulled up in front of the Caffè Castiglione and bought a tray of fifteen cannoli.

Every arancino was as big as a large orange. For a normal person, two arancini would have constituted an already dangerous amount for dinner. Montalbano wolfed down four and a half; Liliana, two.

Before the cannoli were served, the words exchanged in conversation were limited to the bare essentials.

In fact, it was impossible to talk. The arancini tasted

and smelled so good that each person ate in a cloud of ecstasy, eyes half closed, a blissful smile on his or her face.

"These are fantastic! Pure joy! Absolutely incredible!" Liliana exclaimed when she was done.

Adelina smiled at her.

"*Signura mia*, I pu' five o' dem aside, so if you go to th'isspector's house t'morrow, you can taste 'em again."

She would do anything to harm the hated Livia.

At around eleven o'clock Montalbano said he'd promised Signora Liliana they wouldn't stay late.

That was when Pasquale turned to him and said:

"Could I talk to you in private for five minutes?"

They went into Adelina's bedroom. Pasquale locked the door behind him.

"D'jou know I got outta jail three days ago?"

"No. What were you in for?"

"The Montelusa carabinieri caught me. Accomplice to breakin' an' ennerin'."

"What did you want to tell me?"

"There was a rumor goin' round the jail 'at wasn't really a rumor."

"What do you mean?"

"I mean Narcotics's been workin' on Tallarita, an' Tallarita, at least till a few days ago, decided to cooperate with them."

The arancini and cannolo had slowed down the inspector's entire cerebral system.

"And who's Tallarita?"

"He's a big-time dealer, Inspector. An' I'm tellin' you this 'cuz 'is family lives on Via Pisacane."

In a flash Montalbano's brain kicked into high gear.

"Thanks, Pasquà," he said.

"Still feel like talking to me?" Montalbano asked as they were getting in the car.

"Yes. If it's not too late for you . . ."

"Not at all. My place or yours?"

"Wherever you prefer."

"At my place we've got whisky to help us digest; at your place, vodka. The choice is yours."

"I finished the vodka and forgot to buy a new bottle."

"Then we have no choice."

Montalbano drove slowly, weighed down by the arancini. There was little traffic. Liliana sank into her seat, laid her head on his shoulder, and closed her eyes, perhaps succumbing to sleep. She certainly had washed down her arancini with a lot of wine. To avoid waking her, he started going so slow that when he was about to turn left, onto the little road leading to their two houses, the engine stalled.

He started it up again, but then did something wrong. He couldn't figure out what, but the fact was that the car lurched forward through the air, coming a good three or four inches off the ground. And at that same moment,

Montalbano heard a loud crack against the body of the car, but didn't worry, imagining it was probably a stone.

"Oh my God, what was that?" asked Liliana, sitting up and opening her eyes in fright.

"It was nothing, don't worry," said the inspector, reassuring her.

"Listen," she said, "I'm sorry, but I suddenly felt so sleepy."

"Shall we make it another time?"

"If you don't mind . . . Anyway, Adelina's already decided I have to come to your place to eat the rest of the arancini."

"Good for Adelina!"

He dropped her off outside her gate.

"Need a ride into town tomorrow?"

"I don't have to go to work tomorrow. We're closed for mourning. The owner's mother died. Thank you for a lovely evening. Good night."

While it's true that good food is not hard to digest, if you eat a lot of it, you still need some time to digest.

He grabbed a bottle of whisky, a glass, his cigarettes and lighter, and went out on the veranda, but then thought he should call Livia first.

"I just got back," she said.

"Did you go to the movies?"

"No, I went out to dinner with some friends. It was my coworker Marilu's birthday. Remember her?"

He hadn't the vaguest idea who she was. No doubt he'd met her a few times when he was in Boccadasse, but he didn't remember anything about her.

"Of course! How could I forget Marilu? So, was the food good?"

"Certainly better than the awful slop your beloved Adelina makes for you!"

How dare she? Apparently she was spoiling for a fight, but he was in no mood for squabbling. Anyway, if he got upset, it might ruin his digestion. So he decided to give her rope . . .

"Well, I guess Adelina sometimes . . . Actually, tonight I couldn't get anything she made past my lips."

"You see? I'm right. So you went hungry?"

"Almost. I made do with some bread and salami."

"Poor thing!"

Today was ladies' commiseration day, apparently. After a little more conversation, they wished each other good night and hung up.

What happened next took Montalbano so much by surprise that he couldn't tell whether he was dreaming or it was really happening.

He'd just finished his first glass of whisky when he noticed, by the dim light of a slender moon, a human figure walking slowly along the water's edge. When opposite the veranda, the person raised a hand and waved.

Then he recognized her. It was Liliana.

Grabbing his cigarettes and lighter, he went down to the beach. She'd kept walking, but he caught up with her.

"When I got home I didn't feel sleepy anymore," she said.

They walked in silence for about half an hour. The only talking came from the lapping surf like a continuous musical refrain.

Then she said:

"Shall we go back?"

As they were turning around, their bodies lightly touched.

Liliana took his hand as if it was the most natural thing in the world, and did not let go of it until they were back at the veranda. Here Liliana stopped, grazed Montalbano's lips with her own, and headed back towards her house.

Montalbano stood there watching her until her silhouette vanished in the darkness.

One thing he was sure of: if Liliana had decided not to talk to him that evening, it was not because she suddenly felt sleepy, but because what she had to tell him was not something easy to say, and she hadn't had the courage to tell him.

━━━

At eight o'clock the following morning, as he drove past the Lombardos' house, he noticed that the shutters over the bedroom window were still closed. No doubt Liliana was taking advantage of her day off from work to sleep later than usual.

He parked in the station's lot, and in the building's entrance nearly collided with Fazio, who was coming out.

"Where you going?"

"I'm going out to see if I can gather any information on the Via Pisacane bomb."

"Are you in a hurry?"

"Not really."

"Then come with me, there's something I have to tell you."

Fazio followed him into the office and sat down.

"Last night I got what seems like some important information. It was Adelina's son who told me."

He told Fazio what Pasquale had said.

"So the bomb was supposedly intended for Tallarita?" Fazio said when he'd finished. "And it was supposed to mean: watch out, if you cooperate we'll kill one of your family?"

"That's right."

Fazio made a doubtful face.

"What's wrong?"

"I'm just wondering why the Narcotics guys, who certainly must have learned about the bomb, haven't put the family under protection yet."

"Are you sure that's the case?"

"Chief, I drove by their front door yesterday and saw nothing there. No men, no cars."

"Yes, but we should find out whether the Tallarita family is still there; they may have been taken somewhere else."

"No, they're still there, Chief. I'm positive."

Montalbano made a snap decision.

"What did you say his wife's name was?"

"Francesca Calcedonio."

"I'm going to go and talk to her."

"And what should I do?"

"Try to find out from Narcotics exactly what the situation is with Tallarita."

The young man who opened the door was quite good-looking, tall with dark curly hair, an athletic build, and sparkling ebony eyes. Though in shirtsleeves and trousers, he still looked elegant.

"Yes? Can I help you?"

"I'm Inspector Montalbano, police."

In an instinctive reflex, the youth made as if to shut the door in his face, then thought better of it and asked:

"What do you want?"

"I'd like to talk to Signora Tallarita."

Was it just his impression, or did the youth seem slightly relieved?

"My mother's not in. She's out shopping."

"Are you Arturo?"

The kid looked alarmed again.

"Yes."

"Will she be long?"

"I don't think so."

Since the inspector wasn't moving, he added, somewhat reluctantly:

"If you'd like to come in and wait . . ."

He showed him into the dining room, which was modest but clean. In one corner were a small sofa, two armchairs, and the inevitable television set.

"Did something happen to my father?" Arturo asked.

"No, not as far as I know. Why, are you worried about him?"

The kid seemed truly flustered.

"No, why should I be worried about him? I just asked because I have no idea why . . ."

"Why I'm here?"

"That's right."

Arturo got nervous again. The inspector decided to toy with him a little. He made an enigmatic face.

"Can't you imagine?"

Arturo turned visibly pale. It wasn't the reaction of someone who has nothing to hide.

"No . . . I can't . . ."

The front door opened and closed.

"Artù, I'm back," a woman called.

"Excuse me for just a minute," the kid said, taking advantage of the situation and rushing out of the room.

Montalbano heard them whispering animatedly in the entrance hall, and then the mother came in alone.

She looked older than her age, and was fat and panting. She sat down heavily in an armchair and heaved a long sigh of fatigue.

"Are you feeling all right?"

"I have heart disease."

"I'll take only a few minutes of your time."

"It's a good thing Arturo's store was closed today and he didn't have to go to work, or you wouldna found nobody home 'cause my daughter Stella's in Palermo. What can I do for you?"

"Signora, is your husband currently in Montelusa prison serving a sentence for drug dealing?"

"Yes, an' it's not the first time."

"And you live here with your two children?"

"Yes, I do. But the only one who really lives here with me is Arturo, 'cause for the past two years Stella's been going back and forth to Palermo, where she studies at the university."

"Well, what I want to know is whether you or either of your children have recently received any threats."

Signora Tallarita's eyes popped open.

"Wha'd you say?!"

Montalbano patiently started again.

"I want to know whether—"

But Signora Tallarita had heard perfectly well.

"Threats? Us? What do you mean?"

"I don't know, phone calls, anonymous letters . . ."

"What do you want me to say? I swear to you, in this house I never received no threats or anything else."

She thought about this for a second, then suddenly called out so loudly that Montalbano gave a start.

"Artù!"

The kid arrived instantly. Perhaps he'd been outside the door, listening.

"What is it, Ma?"

"At your store in Montelusa, have you received any threats, like phone calls or anonymous letters?"

Arturo was also taken aback.

"Me?! Never! Why would anyone want to do that?"

Mother and son both looked questioningly at the inspector. Who had already prepared an answer.

"We've received some information that the father of an overdose victim is apparently seeking revenge."

The two said nothing. Arturo turned pale.

"Of course I'll inform my colleagues in Narcotics, but in the meantime I would advise some discreet police protection. Therefore I'll need Stella's Palermo address and the name and address of the store where you work, Arturo."

He wrote down the information as they dictated it to him, then said good-bye and left.

He had, however, achieved several results.

For example, it had never even crossed the minds of Signora Francesca and Arturo that the bomb might have been intended for them. And Narcotics had not been in touch with them.

More importantly, why was young Arturo so obviously nervous? Montalbano would have to think about this a little.

"I got lucky," said Fazio. "Five minutes after you left, Aloisi from Narcotics was passing through and came in to say hello."

"Did you ask him about the Tallaritas?"

"Of course. He was totally in the dark."

"He didn't know anything?"

"Nothing. According to him there are no negotiations ongoing with Tallarita."

"Are you sure it's not one of those supersecret operations that Narcotics lov—"

"Nah, he would have given some indication of that."

"So what Pasquale told me is just bullshit?"

"I don't think he lied to you on purpose," said Fazio. "It's possible that somebody who knew about Pasquale's connection to you told him, knowing he would pass the information on to you sooner or later. To throw you off the trail."

"That must be what happened. The Tallaritas meanwhile have no protection and think there's no way that bomb was intended for them."

"You see? It makes sense."

"Yes, but I'm not totally convinced by Arturo, the son."

"What do you mean?"

"In my opinion he's hiding something."

"Want me to see if I can dig anything up?"

"Yes."

The inspector took out the piece of paper with the address and looked at it.

"The clothing store in Montelusa where he works is called All'ultima moda, and it's on Via Atenea, number 104."

"I know the place," said Fazio.

Could you imagine him not knowing?

5

"While you were telling me about Aloisi," the inspector continued, "I was becoming more and more convinced of something."

Fazio pricked up his ears.

"And what's that?"

"Some time ago I happened to see a film by Orson Welles in which there's a scene that takes place in a room entirely made up of mirrors, where the person can no longer tell where he is and becomes completely disoriented, thinking he's talking to someone in front of him when the guy is actually behind him. I think these people are trying to play the same game with us, to lead us into a hall of mirrors."

"What do you mean?"

"They're trying to disorient us. They're doing everything in their power to keep us from understanding who the bomb was really intended for. To be as clear as possible,

I no longer think the bomb was pushed aside towards Arnone's warehouse by chance; I'm convinced the bomb was purposely placed where we found it."

"I'm beginning to understand."

"So they send an anonymous letter to Arnone and at the same time spread the rumor about Tallarita cooperating with Narcotics, with the result that we're always back to square one. We're being led around by their moves, like dogs on a leash. We have to take the initiative ourselves, starting now."

"And how are we going to do that?"

"I'll explain. When I told you to go and have a look at who lives at number twenty-six, Via Pisacane, all you told me was that Carlo Nicotra and two ex-cons live there. And that was because, to your eyes, as a policeman, they were the only three persons of interest. Am I right?"

"Yes."

"And there we probably made a big mistake."

"How?"

"In stopping at those three. What if the bomb was intended for a different tenant, one with no record? Someone above suspicion? Someone we know nothing about yet? And what if they're doing everything humanly possible to prevent us from getting at him?"

Fazio absorbed the blow.

"You're right," he admitted.

"How many families live at number twenty-six?"

"Nine. Three per floor."

"And we stopped at a third of the tenants. So . . ."

"I'll get on it right away."

As soon as Fazio left, the inspector started opening the mail. The first letter was addressed directly to him and had the word PERSONAL written on the envelope.

He opened it and immediately realized that it was an anonymous letter, even though it wasn't handwritten in block letters but typed at a computer.

Cecè Giannino is an unlucky thief. He stole what he shouldn't have and doesn't want to give it back to its rightful owner.

He started laughing. It was the casting out nines of what he'd just finished saying to Fazio. He rang him and told him to come to his office. And when Fazio got there, he handed him the letter.

"Here, read this. They've added another mirror to the mix."

Fazio smiled, too.

When he got to the trattoria, he was the only customer. It was still too early. Enzo was watching television, tuned in to TeleVigàta. Talking on-screen was the station's top newsman, Pippo Ragonese, who didn't like the inspector, and whose feelings were amply returned in kind.

> . . . to return to the bomb that exploded in Via Pisacane, it has come to our attention, through confidential channels, that some willing citizens have indicated a number of possible leads to Inspector Montalbano of Vigàta police, all of which have been shunted aside by the inscrutable public servant. And so, several days after the incident, the brilliant result is that we still don't know who was behind the explosion. Will we have to wait for another bomb to go off before the good inspector wakes up from his long sleep?

"I'll turn it off before that asshole ruins your appetite," said Enzo.

"That's unlikely," said Montalbano. "What've you got?"

He ended up eating a double serving of seafood antipasto in Ragonese's face.

Afterwards he took his stroll along the jetty, but didn't remain seated on the flat rock for very long.

He'd had another idea.

Back in his office, he rang Nicolò Zito, his friend and editor in chief of the Free Channel news department.

"Hey, Nicolò, all well with the family?"

"All's well. What is it?"

"I happened to hear Ragonese's editorial on Tele-Vigàta's midday report."

"Me, too. You must be used to it by now, no? Do you want to respond to him?"

"Indirectly."

"How soon can you get here?"

"As soon as it takes me to drive there."

Just outside Vigàta, he came up against a long queue of stationary cars. He stuck his head out the window. There was a checkpoint of carabinieri up ahead. He cursed a great many of the saints in heaven. It was anybody's guess how much of his time would be wasted. After a few minutes he decided not to wait any longer. He pulled out of the queue to present himself to the carabinieri. He was nearly at the front of the line when an officer came running towards his car.

"Where do you think you're going?"

"I'm Inspector Montalbano."

"Pull over to the left."

"But . . ."

"Pull over to the left and get out of the car!"

The guy wouldn't listen to reason, was pissed off, and was holding a machine gun to boot. Better not make him even angrier.

Montalbano pulled over, got out of the car, and at that moment all hell broke loose.

A big car drove up at a thousand miles an hour, determined to crash through the roadblock. Before throwing himself nimbly on the ground, Montalbano was able to see someone with his arm out the speeding car's window, shooting a revolver or small machine gun at the carabinieri.

He heard the car race past, followed by some bursts of machine-gun fire. The military cops were responding.

Then, after a pandemonium of cars starting and tires screeching and sirens blaring, there was total silence.

He got up. The roadblock was gone. The carabinieri had dashed off in pursuit.

He had the presence of mind to get quickly in his car, start it up, and leave. The other cars were still not moving. The drivers were frozen in fear from what had just happened.

And so he wasn't late for his appointment with Nicolò, whom he found in a rather agitated state.

"I just got a call saying there was an exchange of fire at a carabinieri checkpoint right outside of Vigàta. Do you know anything about this?"

The inspector donned an expression of surprise.

"Really? I didn't see any checkpoint."

If he told the truth, Nicolò was liable to interview him immediately as a witness.

"Let's do this interview right away," the newsman said. "That way I can broadcast it on the seven o'clock edition, then replay it at eight and at midnight. Is that all right with you?"

"That's perfectly fine with me."

"Inspector, first of all let me thank you for having so kindly agreed to grant us this interview. The bomb that exploded yesterday in Vigàta destroyed the metal shutter of an empty warehouse, and therefore did little damage. The danger, however, is that it will do more damage to the reputation of the police."

"How?"

"Apparently on this occasion—contrary to usual practice—a number of witnesses have sent you testimonies that haven't been followed up on. Therefore—"

"Excuse me for interrupting, but I need to set something straight. I haven't received a single testimony—not one—because there weren't any witnesses."

"And what about the letters that were sent to you?"

"I would like to point out that these are anonymous letters. So, you can talk about dutiful citizens if you like, but only up to a point. And they have no proof to

back up their assertions. Just as there's been no confirmation of the rumors that have been cleverly put into
circulation."

"Could you tell us what the letters say?"

*"They contain assumptions or, perhaps more precisely,
conjectures as to whom the bomb might have been intended for."*

"I don't understand for what purpose they were
written."

*"Easy: to throw us off the trail. They present a number
of possible leads in order to confuse us. And this flurry of
activity just confirms my opinion."*

"Can you tell us what that is?"

*"I've no problem telling you. I think there's something
really big behind this bomb. It's not the usual failure-to-
pay-the-protection racket, even though they wanted us to
think this in the early going. Nor is it an attempt to silence anyone who might be thinking of talking. And the
theory that the bomb was to persuade a thief to return
what he'd stolen is just laughable."*

"In conclusion?"

"The investigation is continuing. But I felt it was my duty to reassure our citizens as to the supposed inaction of local law enforcement."

———

"Cat, is Fazio in?"

"Nah, Chief, but 'e called poissonally in poisson like-abouts fifteen minutes ago to say 'e's on 'is way."

"What about Inspector Augello?"

"Nah, 'e ain't 'ere neither. I put a call true to him and a li'l while later 'e went onna scene."

"And where's that?"

"'E din't say. Sorry, Chief, but d'jou know there was an aschange of fires wit' the carabinieri atta roadblock?"

"Yes, I know."

He went into his office and had just grabbed some papers from the pile in order to sign them when Fazio came in.

"Nuttata persa e figlia fimmina."

"Meaning?"

"I went to Montelusa to talk to some people at the clothing store, but it was closed."

"You can go back tomorrow."

"Did you know you have a hole?" Fazio asked out of the blue.

Montalbano instinctively checked his jacket and shirt. Fazio smiled.

"On your car, I mean. I noticed just now when I parked alongside it."

"On my car?!"

They went outside to the parking lot, Fazio leading the way.

The hole was in the right-hand door, at more or less the height of the passenger's seat. A close look revealed that it was clearly from a firearm.

Montalbano opened the door. The bullet had gone straight through the car's body, penetrated the seat back, and come to rest in the stuffing.

Fazio was silent, pale, and worried.

"Don't be alarmed," Montalbano said, smiling. "It was a stray shot; it wasn't aimed at me."

"But how'd it happen?"

He told him about the shoot-out. Fazio heaved a sigh of relief.

"But you can't be driving around with this!"

"What do you suggest?"

"I'll have the car sent to our appointed body shop. I'll tell them to do a quick touch-up job."

"Have them dig out the bullet."

"But they'll have to rip the guts out of the seat!"

"Worse things have happened."

"I'll have Gallo drive you home to Marinella this evening," Fazio decided. "And he'll come and get you in the morning as well. We'll look for a better solution if the repair ends up taking a long time."

"Okay."

Half an hour later Mimì Augello straggled in.

"Where've you been?"

"To Via Pisacane."

"Why?"

"I got a phone call from a man, but he didn't want to give me his name."

"What did he say?"

"That the bomb went off by accident."

This was a new development.

"What do you mean 'by accident'?"

"That's what he said. According to our nameless witness, the bomb was put together by a certain Filippo Russotto, who lives on the third floor of twenty-six, Via Pisacane, and every now and then makes bombs for the Mafia. Supposedly when he was putting the bomb in his car to take it to his clients, something went wrong— exactly what, I didn't quite understand—and so he left the bomb in the street."

"And you believe that?"

"Calm down. Before making any moves, I checked the records. The guy's got a clean one. And so I went and looked at all the names of people associated in any way with bomb explosions. And, in fact, in a trial five years ago, someone claimed Filippo Russotto was the guy who provided the explosives, but he couldn't prove it, and so Russotto got off. And so, just to be sure, I decided to go and check things out."

"And how did they check out?"

"Depends on your point of view."

"Explain."

"Russotto's wife told me her husband's been in Montelusa Hospital for some tests. Apparently he's got something in his lungs. It seems our anonymous caller wasn't aware of this detail."

The attempt to add another mirror to the game had failed.

Fazio returned, and Montalbano brought him up to speed on what Augello had told him.

"They're trying every trick in the book," Fazio commented.

"How'd it go at the body shop?"

"Chief, even for a quick touch-up job, they have to keep the car for four days."

Montalbano cursed.

"So what am I supposed to do?"

"I've already taken care of it. I got you a car that drives exactly the same way as yours. It's outside in the parking lot, the gray car next to mine. Here are the keys."

He set them down on the desk.

"And here's the bullet," he continued.

Montalbano picked it up and looked at it.

"Are you sure this is it?"

"Chief, how many bullets do you think were embedded in your seat?"

"But this is a special bullet from a rifle!"

"So?"

"It can't be from the carabinieri."

"But didn't you tell me you saw someone shooting from the passing car?"

"Yes, but not with a rifle!"

"Maybe you just didn't notice that there was someone else with a rifle."

Montalbano turned pensive. He replayed the scene at the roadblock in his mind and came to a conclusion.

"You know what I'm going to do? I'm going to talk to Lieutenant Vannutelli."

He had Catarella ring the lieutenant, who replied that he would be waiting for him at the headquarters of the carabinieri.

He decided to go on foot. He hadn't had time yet to try out the borrowed car.

"Did you manage to catch them?" he asked the lieutenant.

"No, they got away."

"Did anyone tell you I was there?"

"You were there?!"

Montalbano told him the whole story. And then he showed him the bullet. Vannutelli picked it up, examined it, and looked dumbfounded.

"Where on earth did this come from? People were shooting machine guns and automatic weapons, not rifles."

"That's why I'm here. The entry hole in my car door is perfectly round. The shot must have been fired from a point parallel to my car."

Vannutelli kept looking at the bullet with puzzlement.

"The carabinieri stopped me just as I was beside the first car in the line going towards Montelusa. The shot could only have come from that car, or from the one right behind it."

"What I think you're trying to say is that the guys who drove through the roadblock had armed accomplices, is that right?"

"Precisely."

"Thanks. I'll talk to the marshal who conducted the roadblock and get back to you."

▬

When he got to his office, he called Fazio.

"Have you got any friends in Forensics?"

Montalbano, for his part, had a profound dislike of the chief of Forensics. The mere sight of him gave him a stomachache. And his feelings were returned in kind.

"Sure."

He handed him the bullet.

"Have him look at it in private."

"What do you want to know?"

"Whatever there is to know."

"You in a hurry?"

"No."

"Then I'll take it to Montelusa tomorrow."

As he was about to leave to go home, Lieutenant Vannutelli rang.

"Listen, I had a long talk with Marshal Capua and De Giovanni, the carabiniere who stopped you and remembers you perfectly."

"What did they say?"

"They said your theory doesn't hold water."

"And why not?"

"Because at the moment the speeding car reached the roadblock, Capua was checking the first car in the queue and he's absolutely positive that nobody fired a shot from that car. De Giovanni, on the other hand, right after stopping you, was walking over to the second car and had to squeeze up against it to avoid the speeding car coming through. If anyone fired a shot from that car, it would have struck him."

The argument was airtight.

Then how to explain the bullet hole?

He went into the parking lot, got in the car that Fazio had procured for him, and drove three times around the lot as a test. It felt fine.

So he headed off to Marinella.

6

The lights were on in the Lombardos' house. Therefore Liliana was at home, even though he couldn't see her. Would she be coming to eat the arancini as she'd promised? For no apparent reason, Montalbano had the suspicion that at the last minute she would find an excuse not to come. As he slipped the key into his front door, he heard the telephone ringing. This was something that happened often. It was as though the phone could hear his car approach from a distance and then started ringing at once, so that he wouldn't have time to answer. He tried to move as fast as possible, but when he lifted the receiver he heard only a dial tone.

He went straight to the kitchen, opened the refrigerator, took out the arancini, and put them in the oven, which he then lit and set at a low temperature. Then he went to the bathroom and washed up, came back out, turned on the television, sat down, and watched himself being interviewed by Nicolò. After turning off the set, he started setting the table on the veranda.

When he'd done this, he sat down on the bench, lit a cigarette, and started thinking about what was eating away at him. Where could the shot that struck his car have come from?

The hole of entry spoke quite clearly: there was no splintering; it was clean and formed a perfect circle. The bullet was fired by someone positioned at a perfect right angle to the car and, therefore, if the carabinieri's reconstruction was correct, the shot could only have come from a gunman on the other side of the queue of cars, in the open countryside along the road.

But this wasn't possible, either, because in that case the bullet, before reaching his car, would have ended up hitting one of the cars stuck in traffic.

Unless the gunman happened to have fired the shot from the second floor of a building. But in this case the entry hole should have had an almost oval shape.

There was no explanation.

He looked at his watch. It was already nine fifteen. What was keeping Liliana? Or had she again lacked the nerve to come, as he'd already imagined?

The telephone rang. He hestitated for a moment, unsure whether to answer or not. It might be some hassle that would send his evening up in smoke, just as easily as it might be Liliana herself.

He picked up the receiver.

"Inspector Montalbano?"

"Yes."

"It's Liliana."

"Are you coming?"

"I got as far as your front door, but then I saw a car there that wasn't yours, and so I thought . . ."

"Don't worry, it's mine."

"Why'd you change cars?"

"I had to. I'll explain later."

"Are you alone?"

"Yes."

"I'll be right over."

Montalbano went and opened the door and waited there until he saw her approaching from the road. She was wearing slacks and a blouse, maybe because she had something serious to tell him.

But she certainly was beautiful.

By way of greeting, she shook his hand, a strained smile on her pale face. The inspector took her out to the veranda.

He didn't like the fact that Liliana was so serious and apparently worried, as if preparing to be interrogated. It would be better if she loosened up a little; that would make it easier to talk.

"In the fridge I've got a bottle of that nice wine you liked."

"Sure, why not?"

After she'd drunk half a glass, she sighed deeply, and a bit of color returned to her face.

"Why did you have to change cars?"

Montalbano told her about the shoot-out at the checkpoint, but didn't tell her that the carabinieri had ruled out that the shot could have been fired at that moment.

Now she seemed more relaxed.

"Shall I go and get the arancini?"

"I'll come with you."

"Let's bring our plates with us."

As soon as he opened the oven, a heavenly scent wafted out and overwhelmed their senses.

"Let's do this," said Montalbano. "Since they should be eaten nice and hot, let's just take one each right now, and then we'll come back for reinforcements."

"That sounds wise to me."

They ate them in the twinkling of an eye, finishing the bottle in the process.

"Shall we go?" Liliana suggested.

"Let's."

Liliana opened the oven, put two arancini on the inspector's plate and the only remaining one on hers.

"That way we won't have to come back."

Montalbano grabbed another bottle of wine.

This time they savored them ever so slowly, without talking, but only smiling at each other with their eyes.

Liliana was her usual self again, cordial and pleasant.

The arancini had performed a miracle, lightening the burden of what she had to tell him.

"If you're still hungry, I've got some excellent cheese."

"Are you kidding?"

Liliana helped him clear the table and bring a bottle of whisky, two glasses, and an ashtray outside.

Montalbano noticed when she poured herself a hefty dose.

"Could I have a cigarette?"

She smoked it.

"Could you please turn off the light?"

Maybe she was thinking that she would feel more at ease in the dark.

The inspector turned it off. But between the light from the dining room and the moonlight outside, they could still look each other in the eye.

Liliana began speaking softly.

"I want to explain why I didn't file a report when my car was damaged."

Montalbano held his breath. He knew from experience that any question at all from him, the mere sound of his voice, might at that moment have a negative effect.

"I know who did it," she continued.

This time her pause was longer.

"And I wouldn't want, for any reason in the world, to harm him. It was a childish act, a moment of anger. He won't do anything like it again, I'm convinced of that."

She poured herself more whisky.

"Now comes the hardest part for me."

At that moment the inspector decided to speak.

"Listen, Liliana, as far as I'm concerned, you can stop here. You're under no obligation to explain your actions to me. Especially if we're talking about motivations that I presume are, well, strictly personal."

"But I want to tell you anyway."

She'd suddenly used the familiar form of address, which put Montalbano slightly ill at ease. It lessened considerably the distance he would rather have maintained.

"Why?"

"Because I want to see you as a friend. I would like to be able to ask you for advice, or help . . . You know, I don't have anyone to talk to, to confide in . . . Sometimes the situation becomes unbearable for me . . . And you're a man who conveys such a sense of solidity and self-assurance . . ."

Since they were sitting on the same bench, she slid closer to him, to the point where her body touched his, and continued talking as she lay her head on his shoulder.

Where was she intending to go with this?

"I want you to listen to me. I'm speaking with an open heart, without hiding anything. For two years now, Adriano and I have not had relations. We've become strangers to each other. How this came about I really don't know, but the fact is that it happened. A month after we moved to Vigàta, I found a job in Montelusa, as chief of sales personnel in a large clothing store for both women and men. It's called All'ultima moda. Among the sales personnel there was a young man of about twenty, very good-looking, tall, athletic . . ."

In the inspector's head there appeared a name in giant neon-lit letters: Arturo Tallarita.

But he didn't open his mouth.

"To make a long story short, I resisted his advances. But then I couldn't anymore. After a while I realized I was making a big mistake. He was too young, too impulsive, too possessive . . . And so I forbade him to come and see me anymore. The other evening a friend came and picked me up and brought me home quite late. And the following morning my car was . . . well, you saw it yourself. And so, when I went in to work, I called him aside and . . . he started crying. He confessed and begged me not to report him. And that's the whole story."

No, it was not the whole story. What about the man with the Volvo? But Liliana was no longer talking. She'd put her arm around his shoulders and held him tight.

"I feel so good with you!" she whispered to him, her lips almost touching his ear. All he had to do was turn his head slightly and . . .

The telephone rang.

"Excuse me," he said, freeing himself from her embrace.

It was Livia.

"Are you alone?"

Why did she ask that? What, did she have a sixth sense or something? Did a little bird tell her?

"Yes."

"What's wrong?"

"Nothing."

"Well, aren't we talkative tonight! Can you talk or can't you?"

"I just said—"

"All right, all right, I won't bother you any further."

She hung up.

When he went back out on the veranda, Liliana had stood up and was leaning on the railing.

The magical moment had passed. It was unlikely to return, at least that evening. Montalbano went and stood beside her, firing up a cigarette.

The young woman waited for him to finish smoking it, then said:

"It's late. I'm going home."

"Look, if you want to stay a little longer, I'm not . . ."

Liliana looked at her watch and gave a start.

"I didn't realize it was so late! Oh my God, thanks, but I can't stay; I really have to run!"

Why was she suddenly in such a hurry?

"I'll walk you home."

"No."

That "no" was so sharp that Montalbano said nothing. Liliana went into the house, followed by the inspector.

Standing inside the still-closed front door, she turned and held out her hand.

"Thank you for a lovely evening, for the arancini, and for being so patient with me."

"Tomorrow morning at eight?"

"If it's not too much trouble . . ."

Then all at once she threw her arms around him, kissed him on the lips, opened the door, went out, and closed it behind her.

———

Montalbano went back out to the veranda and sat down.

Dear, beautiful Liliana hadn't told him the whole truth. She'd sung only half the Mass. Which, however, was enough for him to explain Arturo's agitation when he'd shown up at the Tallarita home. Apparently the kid was thinking Liliana had changed her mind and decided to report him for damaging her car. The inspector had to tell Fazio to stop investigating Arturo. It was all clear now.

What remained in total darkness, however, was the way Liliana had behaved with him. She had performed—quite well, he had to admit—the opening moves of a textbook seduction. Tactically perfect. But perhaps it was still too early to try and figure out the reason. He had to wait for another little tête-à-tête before he could see clear on this. At any rate, it was obvious that Liliana wanted him on her side, as an ally.

But against whom?

What was the other half of the Mass?

He made a bet with himself. And having done so, he started laughing.

But before he found out whether he'd won or lost, perhaps it was best to wait a little longer.

And so he poured himself three fingers' worth of whisky and sipped it slowly, taking his time.

Then he went into the house and opened the front door without bothering to turn out the light in the vestibule.

He started walking down the road. When he came within sight of the gate to the Lombardos' house, he felt deeply disappointed. He'd been completely mistaken.

He turned around and headed back home. But after taking three steps, he changed his mind and resumed walking towards the Lombardos' house.

When he got to the gate, he could see the green Volvo parked in the little yard.

Light was filtering through the bedroom shutters.

He'd won the bet.

He slept poorly. It was a mistake not to have taken a nice long walk after eating the arancini.

He woke up at six thirty but needed an entire mug of espresso before he felt in any condition to get as far as the bathroom.

As he was about to enter the shower, he heard the phone ring. It was Fazio.

"Sorry to bother you, Chief, but I wanted to let you know that another bomb went off this morning."

He cursed the saints. Were these people acquiring a taste for it?

"In front of a shop or apartment building?"

"No, in front of a warehouse."

"Anyone hurt?"

"A passerby was injured. He was taken to Montelusa Hospital."

"Anything serious?"

"Nah."

"Is Augello with you?"

"Yessir."

"Then there's no point in me coming. I'll see you later at the station."

Liliana was waiting at the gate. Fresh, well rested, and scented, beaming a big smile brighter than the sun. She wasn't in slacks and blouse, but wearing one of her little home-wrecking dresses.

"Ciao."

As soon as she got in the car, she turned towards Montalbano and kissed him on the cheek.

"Sleep well?" she asked.

"Not too badly; how about you?"

"I slept great. Like a log, despite the arancini."

One could see that it did her good. At least this time she didn't mention babies.

"Shall I leave you at the bus stop?"

"Yes, but first, if you don't mind, I'd like to go for a minute to the Caffè Castiglione. I want to buy some cannoli for a salesgirl. It's her birthday today."

When they got there, she said:

"You come in, too. I'll treat you to a coffee."

One should never refuse a coffee. The café was packed with people eating breakfast, a few of whom greeted the inspector. Liliana ordered ten cannoli at the bar and, as they were drinking their coffee, came so close to him that her hip grazed his.

Then she went over to the cash register to pay while the inspector stayed behind, talking to someone he knew.

"Salvo, do you have two euros by any chance?" Liliana called out loudly to him.

Montalbano said good-bye to his acquaintance, went over to the cash register, gave Liliana two euros, and they got back in the car.

After he'd dropped her off at the bus stop and was heading for the office, all Montalbano could do was smile.

How skillful Liliana had been in showing everyone in the café that she and the inspector were close friends! And perhaps even more than friends.

He would have bet the family jewels that her purse

was full of coins, and she'd done what she did just so she could call him by name in front of everyone.

Little by little, the pieces of the puzzle were starting to fall into place.

"Ahh Chief Chief! Ahh Chief!"

This was the special litany that Catarella intoned whenever there'd been a call from Mr. C'mishner.

"Did the commissioner call?"

"Yessir, 'e did, not ten minutes ago. 'E wannit a talk t'yiz or Isspector Augello, an' seein' as how ya wasn't onna premises yet, I put the call true to Isspector Augello, 'oo was hisself onna premises, afore 'e left immidiotly after talkin' to him, him bein' him, meanin' the same one, hiz-zoner the c'mishner."

Entering his office, the inspector found Fazio already there.

"Do you know what the commissioner wanted?"

"No."

"So, tell me about this bomb."

"Well, Chief, it was exactly the same as the one in Via Pisacane. Stuck inside a cardboard box, which they put in front of the metal shutter of a warehouse in Via Palermo."

"What kind of warehouse?"

"That's just it. It was another empty warehouse."

"Really?!"

"It's been unlet for three months."

"Who does it belong to?"

"It used to belong to a retiree by the name of Agostino Cicarello, a postal employee. He died last month. I talked to his wife. It was his only possession."

"So we have to rule out the protection racket?"

"Of course. And I would add that there's really no chance of a mistake in this case, because the warehouse is isolated. There are no other houses or apartment blocks nearby."

"But what are they trying to prove?"

"No idea," said Fazio, standing up.

"Where are you going?"

"To Montelusa to take the bullet to my friend in Forensics, like you said."

"Ah yes, thanks. And listen, you needn't bother with Arturo Tallarita anymore."

"Why not?"

"Because I found out why he was so nervous when I met him. He was the guy who busted up Signora Lombardo's car."

"And how did you find that out?"

"Signora Lombardo told me herself, last night."

"Ah," said Fazio.

And he didn't budge.

"What is it?"

"When you first spoke to me about Arturo, I thought he might be nervous for another reason."

"Namely?"

"That he knew about the rumor about his father wanting to collaborate with the authorities, and he was scared."

"By the bomb?"

"No, not by the bomb, but by Carlo Nicotra, who lives in the same building."

"What's Nicotra got to do with it?"

"Tallarita senior was dealing for Nicotra."

Montalbano thought about this for a minute.

"Then keep working on Arturo and the other tenants."

7

Midmorning Catarella rang him. It took some effort to pick up the receiver, as his arm had gone stiff, worn out from signing too many papers.

"Chief, 'at'd be summon 'ass not onna line in so much as 'e's onna premisses, a Signor McKennick, an' 'e wants a talk t'yiz poissonally in poisson."

"Wha'd you say his name was, McKennick?"

Catarella didn't answer.

"Have you lost your voice, Cat?"

"Nossir, I c'n talk, but ya gotta unnastan', Chief, I dunno what 'is name is, bu' if ya want, I c'n ask 'im."

"So why'd you say McKennick?"

"'Cuz 'ass what 'e is, a mckennic."

Now the inspector understood. It must be Todaro, the body shop mechanic working on his car.

"Show him in."

Todaro was a tall, big man with red hair, and Montalbano liked him. Despite his bulk, he was rather shy.

The inspector shook his hand and sat him down.

"Tell me everything, Todà."

"I'm sorry, Inspector, but isn't Fazio around?"

"No, he just went out."

Todaro twisted up his mouth.

"Too bad; it woulda been better if he was here."

"Why?"

"So he could confirm what I think he said when he brought me the car."

"And what did he say?"

"That the hole was made onna afternoon of the same day when you got stuck inna middle of a shoot-out wit' the carabinieri and a getaway car."

He decided not to tell him that he hadn't the slightest idea what had really gone down.

"That's correct."

Todaro looked like he didn't know what to do next.

"Well, then, if you confirm it yisself . . . ," he said after a pause, by way of conclusion, and started to get up.

"Wait," said Montalbano. "What did you want to tell me?"

"But now I dunno if iss really true or not."

"Don't worry. Is there something that doesn't add up for you?"

"Well, I wouldn't wanna stick my nose where it don't

belong . . . When you or Fazio says somethin', for me iss the Gospel truth."

The inspector fell prey again to the same doubts that had assailed him after Vannutelli had ruled out the possibility that the rifle shots could have been fired from one of the cars stuck in traffic. Maybe the mechanic had discovered something that might help to explain the mystery.

"Forget about the Gospel and tell me straight."

"Sorry if I ask a quession first . . . Can I?"

Shit, what a pain!

"Go ahead."

"After the shoot-out, did you drive the car a long ways on some country road or unpaved track?"

"Not a chance! I went to Montelusa, parked in a paved lot, and then came back here."

"Ah," said Todaro.

"But what is it you're not convinced about?"

"In my opinion the hole was made earlier."

Montalbano pricked up his ears.

"Are you sure?"

Todaro squirmed in his chair.

"Well, it don't really matter to me one way or another, and iss not like I'm just curious or somethin', but I figgered it was my duty . . ."

"Okay, okay, but tell me please how you arrived at that conclusion."

"The same evening Fazio brought me the car, I got down to work right away and noticed what I just said. I din't tell you sooner 'cause I thought it wasn't none o' my business, but then I made up my mind. An' so I tried to call you last night at the station, but they said you went home, and so I tried you at home, but there was no answer."

The inspector was starting to lose patience.

"All right, but what exactly did you notice?"

"Well, the hole where the bullet entered lifted up a little of the paint all around, but not enough to make it fall. It formed sort of a little pocket. You know what I mean?"

"Perfectly."

"An' so, inside this little pocket, I found a lotta dust, more than coulda accumulated in just half a day."

He had a sharp eye, this mechanic.

"And there's somethin' else," he continued.

"Tell me."

"I've worked on a lotta police cars that got shot up by guns and machine guns an' so on . . . Some bullets, when they pass through a sheet o' metal, they produce a kind of rust on the inside of the hole. But you only start to notice this at least twenty-four hours later. It can't happen in just half a day. And in fact, now you can see it on your car, but it wasn't there when Fazio brought it in to me."

The inspector gave him an admiring look.

"Why don't you get yourself hired as a consultant for the Forensics lab? You're better than a lot of them."

"Thanks. But I think I'm even better workin' in a body shop."

After Todaro had left, Montalbano lingered another half hour in his office, racking his brain over the problem at hand.

It wasn't remotely possible that he was inside the car when the shot was fired. He would necessarily have noticed it; there was no getting around this fact. Unless he had fainted. And he hadn't fainted.

Therefore, according to logic, the shot was fired at his car when he wasn't there.

But when was it fired, then? And where?

Certainly not when the car was parked outside the Free Channel studios. Nor when it was parked outside his house in Marinella. The shot would have woken him up, even in the middle of the night.

Over the past few days he had done nothing but drive back and forth between Vigàta and Marinella, with one excursion to Montelusa.

Where had he parked the car for an extended period of time? Ah yes, outside the front door to Adelina's building.

Could they possibly have shot at the car then?

"May I?" Mimì Augello called from the doorway.

"Come in and sit down. What did the commissioner want?"

"Apparently the unions are organizing a demonstration."

"You call that news?"

"I'm talking about our unions, the police unions. It's going to be a national demonstration, outside of Parliament, to protest the cuts."

"So what's Mr. Commissioner got to do with any of it? Does it bother him? Does he want to prevent it?"

"He just wanted to know what the situation was in our department."

"And what did you tell him?"

"I said I didn't know. Which is the truth."

"You did the right thing. But please do me a favor and try to find out a little more about the situation."

"Why?"

"Because I don't want us to make a bad impression. I want us to be well represented at the demonstration. Got that?"

"Got it," said Mimì.

Fazio came back late, when Montalbano was already thinking about going to eat.

He had an expression fit for a grand occasion.

"Find anything out?"

"I've got something big."

"Talk."

"My friend in Forensics says the bullet is from an unusual kind of shell used with high-precision rifles, the kind with a telescope."

"Like the one used to kill Kennedy?"

"More or less. But he couldn't tell me any more than that."

"Now I've got something to tell you."

And he told him what Todaro, the mechanic, had said.

"The only possible explanation," said Fazio, "is that they shot at your car when you weren't around."

"I came to the same conclusion," the inspector agreed.

"Nor can it be considered a threat or an attempt to intimidate you," Fazio went on. "If I hadn't told you myself, you might never even have noticed the hole. If they'd wanted to send you a clear warning, one that you would be sure to receive, they would have fired a burst from an automatic weapon all along the side of the car."

"And in conclusion?"

"In my opinion, it was a stray shot. Somebody taking target practice. It had nothing to do with you."

"What? So how did it happen? And when?"

Fazio threw up his hands.

"Let's change the subject," the inspector said abruptly. "Didn't you say you had something big?"

"Ah, so I did. Since I was already in Montelusa, I dropped in at the clothing store. No harm in that, since nobody knows me there."

"Not even Arturo Tallarita?"

"I don't think the kid knows me. Anyway, even if he did recognize me, so much the better. That would make him even more nervous. And when people are nervous they say and do stupid things."

"Go on."

"The store is really big. Takes up three floors. Well stocked, too. It has fancy clothes as well as cheap clothes. Very convenient. You should probably have a look there yourself."

The inspector gave him a puzzled look.

"Are they paying you to advertise?" he asked.

"Nah, I'm doing it for free."

What, did everyone want to waste his time that morning?

"When I got there," Fazio continued, "I saw Tallarita serving a customer on the ground floor, and then I saw Signora Lombardo on the second floor. There are at least ten salespersons, male and female. Then I noticed a suit I liked. And a salesman showed me into one of the dressing rooms to try it on. It was the second to the last."

Montalbano huffed.

"Just be patient for a minute. These dressing rooms are all in a row and have only sliding curtains of fabric between them. At the back they each have a large mirror. I'd just taken my trousers off when I heard two people come into the cubicle next to mine, which was the last in the row. I put on the new trousers and looked at myself in the mirror."

"How'd they look?"

Fazio gave him a look as if wondering whether the

inspector was making fun of him, but he said nothing and continued his story.

"Apparently the dividing curtain between the cubicles hadn't been closed all the way, because my mirror was reflecting the image from the mirror in the next cubicle, and—"

"Wait a second. If the mirrors in the cubicles are all one beside the other—that is, all facing the same direction—then your mirror couldn't have reflected the image from—"

"No, it could, in fact, because the mirror in the last cubicle wasn't situated at the back, facing the entrance, as in all the others, but was on the right side. Understand?"

"Perfectly. And what did you see?"

"I saw Arturo and Signora Lombardo kissing. They were completely out of control."

The blow was brutal.

Another game of mirrors. This time not even metaphorical. But it had served to reveal a truth.

Montalbano reacted to this flustering news as only he could.

"So did you buy the suit in the end?" he asked.

He went to the trattoria and ate listlessly, no doubt because of what Fazio had told him. Enzo noticed.

"What's wrong, Inspector?"

"Worries."

Enzo repeated a saying he liked very much.

"The cock and the belly want no worries."

The problem was that you had to carry your worries with you whether you liked it or not. They weren't like an umbrella you could leave at the entrance.

During his walk along the jetty, and when he sat down on the flat rock, all he could think of was Liliana and Arturo kissing on the sly in the dressing room.

It was clear that the girl hadn't sung even half the Mass to him, as he'd believed.

Maybe barely a quarter of the Mass.

And who knew whether, in this labyrinth of lies, it was even true that it was Arturo who had damaged her car?

Or had Fazio perhaps witnessed a sudden, violent re-kindling of the flame, something which in general is rather dangerous?

In the current state of affairs, the inspector found himself faced with a series of occurrences without any apparent reason behind any of them.

To recapitulate:

When, how, and why did somebody shoot at his car?

Why were they putting bombs in front of empty warehouses?

Why had Liliana gone and told him a string of whoppers?

And why had she wanted people to think that she was a close friend of his or maybe more?

Dense fog.

Maybe ten years ago—he thought bitterly—he would at least have been able to outline the beginning of an answer to these questions.

Now, instead, he proceeded in slow motion on everything, one foot up, the other foot down. Like . . .

Like an old man, truth be told.

He could no longer make the sudden sidestep, the one that allows you to advance, that—

Let's not start again with this pain-in-the-ass stuff about old age setting in! Montalbano Two butted in. *You're just fabricating a convenient excuse! And you're also a hypocrite because you are well aware of this. So if you need your own shoulder to cry on, to let yourself go, then go right ahead, be my guest, but only for five minutes, because otherwise you're just busting your own balls and everyone else's!*

At that very moment a possible answer to one of the many questions besieging him popped into the inspector's head.

Thanks for your help, I really appreciate it, said Montalbano One to Montalbano Two.

And he dashed off to the station.

In the parking lot, before getting out of the car, he grabbed a piece of paper and wrote down the license plate number of the green Volvo. If he simply told Catarella the number, the guy was liable to make such a muddle of things that nobody would understand anything anymore.

"Cat, I want to know who this car belongs to. Call up the ACI, the Bureau of Motor Vehicles, God in heaven if you like, but I want an answer within fifteen minutes, max."

Catarella was as punctual as a Swiss watch. He rang the inspector just as time was running out.

"Chief, the atomobile in quession is the propriety o' Signor Addonato Miccichè, who's from 'ere, meanin' to say 'e lives an' resides in Vigàta."

"Did you get the address?"

"Yessir, Via Pissaviacane, nummer twenny-six."

Montalbano leapt out of his chair. That place again?

"Are you sure about that?"

"Abou' wha'?"

"About the address."

"Sure as death, Chief."

Montalbano remained undecided for a moment. Should he call this Miccichè up on the phone or go and meet him in person? He decided on the latter option. People not notified in advance have no time to invent a convenient story.

He got in his car, drove to Via Pisacane, parked, and got out.

Donato Miccichè's apartment was on the same floor as the Tallarita flat, just across the landing.

The inspector knocked, and the door was opened by a man of about sixty in a wheelchair, unshaven, wearing an old pajama top and holding a plaid blanket over his legs.

"Inspector Montalbano, police. Are you Donato Miccichè?"

"Yes."

"I need to talk to you."

"Come in."

The man showed him into the usual living-dining room with a sofa and two armchairs in a corner.

The atmosphere was one of dignified poverty.

"Would you like some coffee?"

"No, thank you, I don't want to take up too much of your time."

"What can I do for you?"

"Do you own a green Volvo with the license plate number XZ 452 BG?"

"Yes." Then, a moment later, "Did somethin' happen?" he asked apprehensively.

"No, it's just a routine check."

Miccichè seemed relieved.

"My insurance is all in order."

"That's not what I'm here for."

"What is it you want to know?"

"Where do you keep the car?"

"I rent a space in a garage just down the street."

"Please give me the address."

"Via Pisacane eleven."

Wouldn't you know it?

"Who usually drives it?"

"Until about six months ago, I always drove it, but then, unfortunately, I couldn't anymore."

"What happened?"

"I got run over by a car while crossin' the street in Montelusa. Broke both of my legs."

"So does one of your family members use the car?"

"My wife don't drive and my two sons don't live here; one works in Rome, the other in Benevento."

"So am I to conclude that your car has been sitting in a garage for six months?"

Miccichè's unease was plain to see. He made as if to say something, then changed his mind and remained silent.

8

Montalbano thought that a bit of encouragement at this point might be a good thing.

"Signor Miccichè, it's not a crime, you know, if you lend it to someone every now and then. Even I sometimes lend my car to my wife or my brother."

He figured it would seem reassuring for him to come off as a cop, yes, but with a family. A person like everyone else.

Miccichè thought it over for a minute before speaking.

"Yeah, I know iss not a crime."

So a bit of encouragement wasn't enough? Should he resort to threats to extract the information from him?

Montalbano assumed a serious expression.

"I ought to remind you that I am a public official, and you are duty-bound to answer my questions."

Miccichè sighed.

"Iss not that I don' wanna answer . . . Iss that iss a very

private matter . . . I wouldn't wanna cause no harm to anyone . . ."

"I formally guarantee you that nothing you say to me will leave this room."

Miccichè finally made up his mind.

"The other apartment on this floor, just across the landing, belongs to the Tallarita family . . . When I had my accident, they really helped me a lot . . . An' I was very grateful for it. One day Arturo, who's their son, came to me an' ast me secretly if he could borrow my car . . . He begged me not to say nothin' to no one, not even his mother . . . He's mixed up with some married woman who lives ousside of town . . . Anyway, since I couldn't use the car anymore an' wanted to sell it, he talked me into keepin' it . . . He would pay for the rent on the garage, the taxes, an' the insurance . . . An' so I said I would sell it to him, but he could take his time payin' me for it. He said no, he didn't want anyone to know that he owned a car . . . And anyway, I liked still havin' the car an' thinkin' maybe one day I might drive it again . . . So, to make a long story short, I gave 'im the keys to the garage, since he uses the car only at night . . ."

Another piece of the puzzle had found its place.

The hypothesis the inspector had formulated on the jetty had proved correct.

Liliana had only one lover: Arturo.

So why was she doing everything in her power to make it seem as if their relationship were over?

If her husband couldn't care less about what she did, and she didn't have another man, what need was there to hide the fact that they were lovers?

On top of that, Arturo, too, was keen on maintaining secrecy. He didn't want anyone else to know.

As far as Arturo was concerned, however, there might be an explanation. In all probability he had a girlfriend in Vigàta, and if his affair with Liliana ever came out, there would be hell to pay with his girlfriend.

While the inspector was driving with his thoughts elsewhere, he realized he hadn't respected the stop sign as he turned onto the Corso. A powerful car coming on at high speed very nearly crashed into him, managing to stop barely an inch away from the broad side of his car. And Montalbano, too, instinctively stopped. At the wheel of the sporty two-seater was a man who just sat there without moving. Montalbano didn't know if the guy was letting him go first, so, just to be safe, he didn't move either.

Then the sports car backed up a little, screeched its tires, took off like a rocket, and vanished in the direction of Montelusa.

The inspector didn't have the time to read the license plate number, but he was fairly convinced he'd just had a glimpse of Signor Lombardo, Liliana's husband.

Was he coming from home?

The moment he was back at his desk at the station, he got an internal call from Catarella.

"'At'd be the Signura Lombardi onna line, Chief, wantin' a talk t'yiz."

"Lombardi or Lombardo?"

"Lombardi."

"Are you sure?"

"I'm sure she got a pluralistick name, Chief."

Montalbano was right to doubt him. Naturally, her name was not pluralistick, but singularistick, and the person on the line was indeed Liliana.

Who immediately started talking as soon as she heard the click of the call being put through, so that the inspector barely got out so much as a syllable.

"Hel—"

"Ciao. Listen, Salvo, I'm sorry to bother you at work, but I couldn't help it."

"It's no bother at all!"

"I have a proposal for you."

"Let's hear it."

She giggled.

"First you have to say yes."

"How can I say yes if I don't know what it is?"

"You have to trust me."

That was the last thing one should do with someone like Liliana. The lady had shown herself capable of leading him down the Corso and into a crowded establishment and behaving as if they had just gotten out of the same bed. And so? What was happening to him? So now he was starting to fear a woman's ruse, and a rather ingenuous one at that? The problem was that he liked everything about this woman. Even her playacting.

"All right, then. Yes."

"Since I can get off work an hour early today, this evening I can return your favor and invite you to dinner. Are you free?"

She was offering him an excellent opportunity not to come. He could invent whatever excuse he liked . . .

Yes or no?

Make up your mind, Montalbà. Don't forget all the bad that befalls the indecisive, from Buridan's ass to Hamlet.

"Yes."

"So you'll come? Don't forget you've already said yes to me, so if you say no now, you'll be going back on your word."

"I'll come."

"Promise?"

"Promise."

"You have no idea how happy that makes me."

And she sent him an audible kiss through the telephone cable.

"Listen, Liliana, sorry, but I think I saw your husband just a little while ago."

Another giggle.

"That's possible."

"So will I meet him tonight?"

"Of course not! He must have dropped by the house to pick up something he needed. Don't worry, we'll be alone, just the two of us."

It was quite likely that phone call was made in the presence of others.

Liliana was speeding things up. What need was there for her to do that? What other lies would she tell him?

Speaking of which, was her husband always just passing through? Didn't he ever stay home for a few days?

This question brought a number of others along with it, like cherries falling from a tree.

Did this computer representative with exclusive rights for a given brand across the whole island have a sample collection?

And did he have a stock of computers that he could leave with companies and prospective buyers to try out?

And where would he keep such a stock?

At his house in Marinella?

And why had all these questions about Liliana's husband suddenly come to mind?

What was their purpose?

And what should he bring to Liliana's?

Roses or cannoli?

You know perfectly well that you've already opted for cannoli, interrupted that pain-in-the-ass, Montalbano Two.

And wouldn't it be better to be done with all these questions, which were giving him a headache?

He rang Fazio and told him to come to his office.

"What were you doing?" the inspector asked him.

"Nothing. I was just asking myself why these people keep putting bombs in front of empty warehouses."

"You're telling me! I've been racking my brains over that. Did you come to any conclusions?"

"Nah."

"Me neither."

"Did you want something?"

"Yes. I called you in to ask you whether you knew that Arturo has use of a car."

"No. I asked around. I even inquired at the ACI. He doesn't seem to own a car."

"That's because the car he uses isn't his. He borrows it. The car he drives is a green Volvo."

Fazio goggled his eyes.

The inspector told him everything.

"So La Lombardo presumably has only one lover?" Fazio asked.

"So it seems."

Fazio remained pensive.

"Then I don't understand why she told you she'd broken up with the kid."

"Maybe because she's doing everything possible to hook up with me. And she would like to convince me that the whole pie is for me and that I don't have to share it with anyone, not even her husband."

Fazio gave him a bewildered look.

"But why would she do that?"

Montalbano pretended to get upset.

"What do you mean, 'why would she do that?' What about my manly charm? My good looks? My intelligence?"

Fazio wasn't buying it.

"Chief, if it was only a matter of charm and stuff like that, you wouldn't be telling me all this. You know perfectly well that the lady is acting this way because she has a specific purpose in mind, something other than sleeping with you."

He was sharp, no doubt about it.

The telephone rang.

"Chief, 'at'd be Signura Lombardi onna line again."

"Put her on."

He put on the speakerphone so Fazio could also hear.

"Hello, Liliana, what is it?"

"I forgot that I don't have any food at all in the house. I have to go shopping."

"Shall we postpone it for another time?"

"I wouldn't dream of it. On the contrary, I wanted to ask you to lend me a hand."

"I'd be happy to. How?"

"Well, I'll be coming into town on the Montelusa bus in about fifteen minutes. If you could pick me up and come with me to do some shopping . . ."

The inspector looked at Fazio, who remained expressionless. He'd come this far, might as well go all the way . . . He decided to play along.

"All right, I'll be there. Ciao."

He hung up. Fazio looked at him questioningly.

"She wants to put on a little show with me, you see? So that half the people in town think we have a close relationship, maybe even an intimate one. That way she can make it seem like she doesn't have another man—namely, Arturo."

"All right. But who are they trying to hide from? Who are they afraid of? Certainly not the husband. And Arturo's not married."

"And why am I going to dinner at her place tonight? To try and find out just that."

When he got to the stop, the bus hadn't arrived yet, so he stepped out of the car to smoke a cigarette. There were already about ten people waiting for the bus, which after a fifteen-minute stop would depart again for Montelusa.

The stage was set.

The first thing Liliana did when she got off the bus was to run towards him with open arms and cries of joy, embrace him, and kiss him on the cheeks.

So that Montalbano was immediately hated by the three or four men who witnessed the scene.

Then the show began.

At the baker's she held him arm in arm the whole time. At the grocer's she kept an arm around his waist the whole time. At the butcher's she found a way to steal a kiss.

"I'm done."

"I'd like to buy some cannoli myself."

"All right, I'll come too."

She didn't want to miss the chance. She made it so that when they entered the café they were holding hands, with her looking at him as if he were Sean Connery in the days of 007.

Montalbano thought she could have saved time and effort by publishing an ad announcing to one and all that they were lovers.

"And now you're going to drive me home and go back to your place, and we'll see each other again at nine, not before."

"Okay."

He felt half amused, half annoyed. Amused because he wanted to see how far Liliana would take this dangerous game, and annoyed because she apparently took him for a complete moron ready to damn himself at the mere sight of her thighs.

The phone rang, and he went to pick up. It was Nicolò Zito.

"Salvo, I tried you at the station but they said you were at home and so . . . Am I bothering you?"

"No, Nicolò. What is it?"

"I don't know where to begin . . ."

"Is it something serious?"

"I dunno. Listen, I'm going to ask you a question, but I don't want you to think I'm crazy."

"I won't."

"If I hadn't called you right now but, say, three or four hours from now, would I be bothering you?"

What had got into the guy? What kind of question was that?

"I probably wouldn't have answered the phone."

"Why not?"

"Because I would have been out. I have to go and see someone."

"Male or female?"

But what did it matter to Zito? Nicolò, however, was too good a friend; there must be something behind this phone call.

"Female."

"Far from Marinella?"

"No, just a stone's throw from my house."

"Listen, don't take this the wrong way . . . Just asking

you these questions is making me sweat . . . Is this some
sort of . . . well, amorous tryst?"

"Nicolò, this is where I stop talking. Now it's your
turn."

"I have to tell you something I found out by chance
from my cameraman . . . He's friends with another cameraman who works for TeleVigàta, and tonight they were
supposed to go out dancing . . . but the guy called my
colleague to say he couldn't make it tonight, because he
had to cover an important story, a real scoop, somewhere
around Marinella . . ."

"So?"

"I don't know why, but I thought it might concern
you . . . You're the only person living in Marinella who
could possibly be of any interest to the folks at TeleVigàta."

"Thanks, Nicolò. You're a real friend."

He hung up, feeling a slight bitter taste in his mouth.
Part of him believed it, and part of him didn't. But
shouldn't he probably protect himself regardless?

He rang Fazio.

They talked a long time.

And they came up with a plan.

The gate was closed. She came and opened it, then took
care to close it again. She was wearing a dress that looked
like the winner of a contest to see which dressmaker could
use the least amount of fabric and still make a dress.

Even though there were no onlookers, she kissed him on the mouth and led him inside, holding him by the hand.

She was smiling and stepping so lightly she seemed to be flying.

A picture of true happiness.

As might be expected, she had set the table on the veranda.

But there was a lot more light outside than the previous time, which was disturbing.

Liliana intercepted Montalbano's glance at the wall sconce and explained.

"The bulb burned out and all I could find in the house was this hundred-watt bulb."

So while we're eating, thought the inspector, *the mosquitoes will be eating us*.

They didn't sit across from one another. Liliana had put out two chairs side by side.

"This way I can look out at the sea, too," she said.

Not far from shore there was a boat with two fishermen on it. What on earth could they have been fishing for at this hour so close to the beach?

It was very hot outside.

The tête-à-tête got off to an unromantic start. As they were looking at each other and smiling, Montalbano suddenly slapped Liliana's left shoulder, and she immediately followed with a quick cuff to the side of the inspector's head.

The first two mosquitoes had fallen on the field of battle, but reinforcements by the thousands were on their way.

They were barely halfway through the antipasti and Liliana's bare shoulders and arms were already covered with pink mosquito bites. They couldn't go on this way.

"Listen," said Montalbano, "I think all the mosquitoes in the province are gathering here. The light is too bright. I should go and get another light bulb from my house, or else replace this one with something from your dining room."

"Just turn it off," Liliana said with irritation.

Montalbano obeyed. As a result, they were plunged into total darkness, so that they barely knew where their mouths were anymore. The inspector felt like laughing.

How was Liliana going to remedy the situation, which was threatening to turn into a farce?

"The only solution is to move everything into the dining room," she finally suggested, reluctantly.

Apparently the dining room was not the preferred battlefield for her war plans.

And so they started going back and forth, carrying bottles, dishes, glasses, silverware, tablecloth, and napkins.

On his last journey out to the veranda, Montalbano noticed that the two fishermen were pulling their boat ashore. Maybe they'd figured they wouldn't catch any more fish that evening.

9

Inside the house, however, the heat was almost unbearable. They finished the antipasti with the help of some ice-cold white wine, which went down like a dream.

The wine gave Liliana the strength to make an attempt to end the stalemate.

"It pains me just to look at you," she said at one point, smiling. "How can you stand it? Take off your jacket and unbutton your shirt, or you're going to melt like a ball of ice cream."

It wasn't true. The inspector would hardly have broken a sweat even at the equator, but he concurred.

"You're right. Thanks," he said.

He remained in shirtsleeves with his collar unbuttoned. And what was she going to do now? Start some sort of game of strip poker?

Since she wasn't doing anything, he decided to provoke her.

"And what about you?"

"I can still hold out as I am."

She was saving her secret moves for later, when the atmosphere would be more conducive.

She got up from the table and brought back a platter of pasta in salmon sauce.

Montalbano's heart gave a flutter. If the pasta was overcooked, he would be unable to swallow it. Instead, to his relief, he immediately found that, while not superb, the pasta was at least edible.

And it helped them to polish off a second bottle of wine.

Eating the pasta hadn't been easy, however, since every so often, as he was bringing a forkful to his mouth, Liliana would suddenly grab his hand, bring it to her lips, and kiss the back of it.

When they were done, Montalbano helped her bring the empty plates and silverware into the kitchen.

For the second course, she'd prepared two slices of beef in a hot sauce that he'd never tasted before.

The spicy sauce called for more wine. Montalbano couldn't tell whether Liliana was beginning to feel its effects or was just pretending.

First came the giggles.

"Your moustache. . . . heeheehee! . . . Look at this little crumb . . . heeheehee!"

Then she dropped her fork and the inspector bent down to pick it up.

As he was crouching, she put her naked foot on his back, between the shoulder blades.

"I dub thee knight of my . . ."

Montalbano never found out what sort of honor she was bestowing on him because she started to fall out of her chair and didn't finish her sentence.

But she pulled herself quickly back up, announcing that she couldn't stand the heat any longer and had to change her clothes because her sweat-dampened little dress was bothering her.

"I'll be back in five minutes," she said, heading for the bedroom door.

But after taking three steps, she turned around, approached Montalbano, who in the meantime had stood up out of politeness, wrapped her arms around his waist, put her mouth on his, and pressed it there, opening her lips ever so slowly.

The kiss was a long one.

To say that Montalbano went along with it only out of his sense of duty as a policeman would have been stretching things.

In fact, his body started to act the way the Garibaldini were said to have acted when they sprang to the attack before the general had ever given the order.

His hands, for example, independently of his will, descended as far as the young woman's posterior globes.

She then took him by the hand and, staggering slightly, led him into the bedroom.

She turned on the light. The window was open.

In a flash she'd taken off her little dress. She wasn't wearing a bra, and had on a purely hypothetical pair of panties.

She lay down on the bed and opened her arms toward Montalbano, smiling.

At this point Montalbano realized he was utterly lost.

His right foot made one step towards the bed, despite the fact that his brain was ordering him with all its authority to stay put and not move.

The left foot followed its colleague with equal enthusiasm.

Only divine intervention could save him now from the abyss into which he was about to plummet.

"Come on! What are you waiting for?"

The immediate effect of her voice was to induce the inspector to leap forward, in that both his feet responded simultaneously to the invitation.

Probably only Saint Anthony could have resisted.

And Saint Anthony, heeding the call, promptly intervened.

Montalbano's cell phone, which he'd transferred from his jacket to his trouser pocket, started to ring.

The return to reality was so violent that the inspector gave a sort of cry of pain.

It was Fazio.

"We caught 'em and are bringing 'em in to the station," he said. "Now you can pick up where you left off, if you want."

Was there a note of sarcasm in his last statement?

"No, I'll be right over," said Montalbano.

Then, turning to Liliana: "I'm sorry, but I have to go."

"Are you crazy? Do you really mean that?"

Liliana had sat up and was glaring at him so intensely that if he'd kept still for another second he would have caught fire.

He didn't answer, but merely ran and grabbed his jacket, jumped down from the veranda, bounded across the beach to his house, got in the car, started it up, and drove off.

It took him little more than a quarter of the time it usually took him to go from his house to the station, but he wasn't sure whether he was driving so fast because he wanted to escape Liliana or because he was so anxious to interrogate the two suspects.

While waiting for him, Fazio paced back and forth in the station parking lot, which was practically deserted.

The inspector gave him a questioning look.

"It's too hot inside," Fazio explained.

"So where are they?"

"We put them in a holding cell. I sent Gallo home to bed."

"You did the right thing. Did they give you any trouble?"

"The usual sort of stuff."

"Where'd you nab them?"

"Right outside the bedroom window. They'd climbed over the gate."

Montalbano marveled.

"Right outside the window? How come I didn't hear anything?"

Fazio answered a bit awkwardly.

"Well, we made some noise, Chief, but you were . . . I think your thoughts were elsewhere at that moment."

Good thing there wasn't much light in the parking lot, or Fazio would have noticed that the inspector was blushing.

They went inside, to Montalbano's office. Right in the middle of his desk, in full view, was a brand new video camera.

"They filmed you with this," said Fazio. "If you want to see yourself . . . it's got a built-in monitor."

Montalbano's blood froze. Did he really have to see himself playing the star of a tacky porno flick? *The Inspector and the Deep-Throat Femme Fatale . . . Wet Investigations . . .* He felt too out of breath to say yes.

So he just nodded assent, as his legs were giving out from under him, and he collapsed in a chair.

Fazio, pretending not to notice his discomfort, came up to him and set the video cam down in front of him.

"You ready?"

"Y . . . es."

Fazio pushed a button.

The filming started at the moment Liliana turned on the bedroom light.

As soon as she took off her dress and lay down in bed, the motherfucking sonofabitch of a cameraman zoomed in on the inspector's face.

Oscar for Best Actor.

His expression was a cross between that of a starving dog being shown a piece of meat and that of chaste Joseph trying to escape the clutches of Potiphar's wife.

As his eyes were about to pop out of their sockets, his lips moved like those of a small child about to start crying.

To say he looked ridiculous wouldn't be saying enough. If these images had been broadcast, all of Vigàta would be laughing behind his back.

But he didn't have to drink the bitter cup down to the dregs. The filming stopped just as he was taking his first step towards the bed like a robot starting up.

Matre santa, how embarrassing!

Good thing they hadn't filmed the kiss in the dining room!

"Have you . . ." he began.

The voice that came out of his mouth sounded bizarre, like that of a turkey-cock. He cleared his throat and started over.

"Have you identified them?"

"Yessir. The cameraman's name is Marcello Savagnoli

and his assistant is Amedeo Borsellino. They both work full-time for TeleVigàta. You want me to bring them in here?"

Would he be able to control himself and not start punching them and kicking them in the balls?

Maybe, maybe not. Whatever the case, he could try.

"All right."

Savagnoli—medium height, open shirt, gold crucifix in a thicket of chest hair, gold bracelet—had the face of a scoundrel, while Borsellino looked genuinely scared.

Before anyone said anything, the cameraman sat down and sneered at Montalbano.

"One at a time," the inspector said to Fazio. "I'll interrogate Borsellino afterwards."

As Fazio was going out with the assistant, Montalbano stood up, went over to Savagnoli, and, smiling affably, said:

"Would you please stand up?"

As soon as the man was on his feet, he dealt him a swift kick in the balls. Savagnoli gasped for air and fell to the floor like a sack of potatoes, writhing and groaning.

"Not a peep!" Montalbano threatened.

Then he went and sat back down.

"What happened?" asked Fazio, coming in.

"Dunno," the inspector said with a cherubic face. "He must have had a sudden bellyache. Sit him back down and give him a glass of water."

When Savagnoli recovered, his attitude had entirely changed. He kept his eyes lowered, was sweating, and no longer looked like a scoundrel.

"How did you catch them without their noticing?" the inspector asked Fazio.

They'd already prearranged part of the answer to the question before he went to Liliana's. But he wanted Savagnoli to hear it.

"We were just conducting our routine evening patrol," Fazio began, "when we saw two individuals scale the gate to a house in Marinella, enter the yard, and position themselves outside an open window. We waited and watched, out of view, to see what they were doing. And we finally intervened when we saw that they were secretly filming what was going on inside that room."

The inspector looked over at Savagnoli.

"That should be enough to charge them with a crime, I should think," he said. "Don't you agree? Violation of property, violation of privacy, intent to blackmail . . ."

"I was only following the orders of my employer, Mr. Ragonese," the cameraman replied.

"And what orders were those?"

"He said there was a big scoop in the making. He'd received an anonymous phone call."

"At what time did you arrive at the scene?"

"A little before you did. We noticed there was a lot of light outside on the veranda . . ."

"You didn't know this beforehand?"

"How could we have known?"

"Go on."

"We saw a boat beached nearby, so we put it out in the water and pretended we were fishermen. We were hoping things would heat up quickly. But after a while you and the lady went into the dining room. There was no way we could film you in there. And so we forgot about the boat, went around the house, climbed over the gate, and waited in the dark outside the bedroom window in the hope that sooner or later . . ."

Between the heat and the things the guy was saying, Montalbano couldn't stand it any longer. He felt like he was going to throw up and didn't want to hear anything else.

He sprang to his feet. Everyone looked at him.

"Tell Mr. Ragonese that, if he knows what's good for him, he'll be here at the station tomorrow morning at nine," he said to Savagnoli.

Then to Fazio:

"Confiscate the video cam, write up a report, then release these assholes. I'm going home."

There were two points in Liliana's favor, Montalbano reflected on his way home.

She had not put in the hundred-watt bulb to facilitate the filming. And she had made no prior arrangement with the cameramen.

So was she part of it or wasn't she? And, if so, to what degree?

Or was she totally innocent of the trap that had been set for him, which luckily hadn't worked out?

In other words, did the person who made the phone call to Ragonese want to entrap just him, or Liliana as well?

Driving past the Lombardos' house, he noticed that it was all dark. Liliana must have gone to bed, mad as hell at him.

He sat outside for a while, waiting for his agitation to pass. He'd dodged a bullet, thanks to Nicolò. Ragonese would probably have aired the scoop ad infinitum.

But, when you came right down to it, would it really have been such a scoop? There certainly wasn't anything illegal about his actions, though he, much more than Liliana, would have been publicly disgraced. The commissioner would surely have had him transferred. And perhaps, in the final analysis, that was the real purpose of the scoop. He went to bed, but tossed and turned a great deal before finally managing to fall asleep. The heat was the main reason, of course, but every so often the image of Liliana with her arms open threw gasoline on the fire.

The following morning, Liliana was not waiting outside the gate at eight. There was no sign of life inside the house. She must have taken the city bus to work. It had to have been the first time she'd been rejected by a man. He probably wouldn't be seeing her again, except perhaps by chance—unless her unexplained need to have him as a friend somehow proved stronger than her resentment over being slighted.

Indeed, things had not gone the way he'd wanted them to go the previous night, and he'd failed in his intent to discover Liliana's reasons for acting out this whole song and dance with him.

At nine on the dot, he got a call from Catarella.

"Chief, 'at'd be 'at 'ere's a Signor Fragolesi onna premisses sez 'e got a pointment wit' yiz . . ." (It must have been Ragonese) " . . . anna lawyer called Calalasso 'oo'd be 'ere wit 'im, 'im bein' a foremintioned Signor Fragolesi."

"Show them in and get me Fazio, too."

The lawyer's name was Calasso. Montalbano knew and respected him. He didn't hold out his hand for Ragonese to shake, and the newsman responded in kind. The two men were sitting down as Fazio appeared with some papers in his hand. The reports from the night before.

"Shall I go first?" Montalbano asked.

"You have to, since you're the prosecution," said Ragonese.

"No," the inspector retorted, "the prosecution will be represented by the prosecutor, for whom I will immediately draft a report after this meeting, which, if your attorney agrees, will not be set down in writing."

"I agree," said the lawyer.

"So, here's what happened. Yesterday evening, Inspector Fazio, here present, and Officer Gallo, conducting their normal patrol, saw two individuals climb the gate outside a house in Marinella, enter the yard, and position themselves outside an open window. Shortly thereafter one of them started filming what was happening inside the room. At this point Fazio and Gallo decided to intervene. All this was written down in a report last night and confirmed by the two persons arrested. If you'd like to read it . . ."

Fazio made as if to hand it to the lawyer, but the attorney stopped him.

"There's no need," he said.

"I don't agree," said Ragonese.

"You don't agree with what?"

"That the two policemen were just there by chance. I am more than certain that Inspector Montalbano was warned in advance by someone at TeleVigàta and that—"

"Would you like to intervene, counsel?" Montalbano asked. "Would you please explain to your client that he's making an assertion with no rhyme or reason to support it? And that, in any case, that's not the problem here?"

Ragonese was about to open his mouth again, but Calasso said dryly to him:

"Please speak only when I tell you to."

"Okay," the inspector resumed. "Savagnoli, the cameraman, stated in the report that he was acting on orders from Mr. Ragonese, here present, who apparently sent the clandestine film crew based on information he received from an anonymous phone call."

He paused for a moment, then slowly uttered a statement he'd prepared in advance, and upon which all his hopes rested.

"A phone call which Mr. Ragonese, naturally, is in no position to prove actually happened, and which, therefore—"

"Just a minute," said Ragonese.

And before going on, he glanced at his lawyer, who nodded in agreement.

Montalbano's face was blank, but he was rejoicing inside. He'd been hoping against hope that Ragonese would let him hear the phone call.

"Actually, I *can* prove that the phone call took place," Ragonese said triumphantly.

"How?"

"I customarily record all incoming phone calls."

He pulled a small tape recorder out of his pocket, placed it on the desk, and turned it on.

A good hundred or more bells started pealing festively in Montalbano's head.

10

As the tape started, Ragonese, convinced he'd scored a point in his favor, looked at the inspector triumphantly, not realizing he'd fallen straight into a trap.

The first thing they heard was the telephone ringing over and over, then the sound of the receiver being picked up, then a voice, recognizable as Ragonese's:

"Hello?"

Izziss . . . Izziss TeleVigàta?

"Yes."

Izziss the news desk?

"Yes."

'Ooziss talkin'?

"Ragonese, the editor in chief."

Yer jess the man I wanna talk wit'. Lissen up . . . an' lissen close. T'night, 'rounnabout eight thirty, Isspecter Mon . . . Montalbano's gonna go see Signura Lombardo 'oo lives inna house ri . . . right nexta his, in Marinella. Got that? Or d'ya wan' me to repeat it? T'night Isspecter Mon . . . Montalbano's gonna—

"Yes, yes, I got that, but I don't see how the thing could be of any interest to us. And who is this calling, may I ask?"

Fuhgeddabout 'oo's callin'. Jess lissen to what I gotta say. The way tings is goin', iss guaranteed the two's gonna end up fu . . . in bed together. An' you c'n film 'em when they's fuckin'. Whattya say, ya intersted?

"Well, yes, thank you for the valuable information. I really appreciate it, but . . ."

Try not to waste any time.

The call was cut off.

Montalbano, who had felt his blood boiling as he was listening, glared indignantly at Ragonese.

"I want you to leave my office this instant without another word. Counsel, I advise you that in my report I intend to charge your client with attempted blackmail."

"It was a scoop, not blackmail!" Ragonese protested.

Then he started yelling.

"This is an attack on freedom of information! On the proper functioning of the press! I intend to publicly denounce this action on your part!"

"Don't raise your voice! You should be ashamed of yourself! You're not a journalist, you're an extortionist!"

"I demand the immediate restitution of my station's video camera and all recorded materials!"

"You can address your request through the proper channels," said the inspector. "And I advise you not to destroy the recording of the telephone conversation, since you can be sure the prosecutor will subpoena it. And now I ask you please to vacate the premises. Fazio, please show these gentlemen out."

Fazio went out with the two as the inspector circled his desk four times, trying to calm down.

Naturally a charge of blackmail would never hold up. He'd only said it in a moment of rage.

But this very fact made his blood boil even more.

Fazio was back in a flash. He was panting heavily, as if he'd been running hard.

"Ah Chief!"

He sounded exactly like Catarella whenever the c'mishner called. Montalbano got scared.

"What is it?"

"I recognized the voice in the recording!"

"Are you sure?"

"Absolutely certain. Didn't you notice how he stammered every so often?"

"I did. So who is it?"

"Nicotra. Carlo Nicotra."

Montalbano felt bewildered. He sat down.

"Nicotra? The one who oversees the drug trade for the Sinagras? And who lives on Via Pisacane?"

"That's the one."

"And what's he got to do with any of this?"

It was an entirely unexpected complication. A new element that might shed light on a lot of things or else cast them into a permanent fog.

The inspector felt as if he were in a boat without oars in the middle of a storm at sea. But his disorientation didn't last long.

"Let's think about this for a minute."

Fazio sat down.

Think about it? Of course, they could and should think about it. But it would take a good long while.

"The first and most natural question that comes to mind," said Montalbano, "is: How did Nicotra find out about my dinner with Signora Lombardo?"

Fazio squirmed uncomfortably in his chair, then said:

"Chief, I can tell you what I think, but you mustn't take offense at what I say."

"Are you kidding me?"

"It's something that just came to me out of the blue, without me having to think about it. Don't you think it might have been Signora Lombardo herself who informed Nicotra?"

The inspector remained silent. The same thought had flashed through his mind as well, but he'd discarded it at once. Still, it was best to find out why Fazio'd had the thought in the first place, so he asked:

"Are you trying to tell me that you assume Lombardo and Nicotra know each other?"

"No, I didn't make myself clear. The lady doesn't know Nicotra, I would bet the house on it. But you can be sure Arturo Tallarita knows him. His father, the one who's in jail, has worked for Nicotra and still does. And it's possible the kid was present when La Lombardo phoned you."

Montalbano drew the logical conclusion.

"So, in your opinion, Arturo is aware of Liliana's designs on me?"

"Yessir."

"So why would he just sit back and let her cheat on him?"

"'Cause they have an agreement."

This was something that hadn't even remotely occurred to him. But there were some grounds for the assumption. Something to work with.

Fazio continued.

"They're using you to make it look like there's nothing between them anymore, like they've broken up. And what better way to make a show of it than to have a video aired on TV?"

"When you put it that way, it seems convincing. I think you're right. But I also think that Arturo acted on his own initiative in informing Nicotra, without letting Liliana know."

"So you're convinced the girl didn't know anything?"

"I'm almost convinced, after what Savagnoli told us. Before, I saw things differently. I thought Liliana was in it up to her neck. But there's still something in your argument that doesn't add up for me."

"And what's that?"

"What need was there for Arturo Tallarita to get Nicotra involved by having him make the phone call? He could have phoned Ragonese himself, whether or not Liliana was in on it."

"That's true."

They remained silent for a spell, thinking.

"Unless . . ." the inspector said all at once.

"Unless?"

"You said once that Arturo, knowing that people were saying his father was planning to collaborate with the authorities, was probably afraid of how Nicotra would react. Is that right?"

"Yes."

"Now, say Nicotra has Arturo under surveillance and therefore has someone inside the big clothing store in Montelusa working as his informer. Might this person not have overheard Liliana's phone call to me and then informed Nicotra?"

"It's a plausible hypothesis. However . . ." Fazio began cautiously.

They both seemed to be walking on eggshells. Before venturing to say anything, they had to weigh their words.

"However?" the inspector pressed him.

"I still don't see what Nicotra gets out of this," Fazio concluded.

"Look, if a scandal broke out, I would definitely be transferred. That'd be already a lot."

"In all honesty, it doesn't seem like enough to me. Underneath it all there's got to be something bigger."

All things considered, it didn't seem like enough to Montalbano either.

Then, all at once, he had a crazy idea.

"And what if the scoop wasn't supposed to harm me?"

"You mean what if it was supposed to harm the lady instead?"

"In a sense, yes . . ."

"Explain."

"Let's say Arturo knows nothing about Liliana's behavior with me, and that she's acting the way she is for reasons we don't know yet. Upon seeing those images, how would the kid react with his lover? Surely he would leave her. Maybe this is the result Nicotra wanted."

Fazio shook his head skeptically.

"Chief, just think for a second. Why would Nicotra want to make trouble between Liliana and Arturo? There's no indication anywhere that he's gay and has a relationship with the kid!"

This was also true.

Montalbano sighed.

"I don't understand any of this anymore" was his bitter conclusion.

When he entered the trattoria, the inspector noticed *cavaliere* Ernesto Jocolano sitting alone at a table.

The cavaliere was a tiny, skinny man of about seventy with thick eyeglasses, who for reasons unknown came to eat at Enzo's once a month.

The next two hours thus promised to be entertaining, because the cavaliere never missed an opportunity to quarrel with Enzo over the most harebrained pretexts imaginable.

Having just sat down, he took the napkin off his plate, picked up the plate, brought it to his nose, and started breathing deeply. Then he put the dish back down on the table.

"Enzo, come here at once!"

He had a very high-pitched voice that was hard on the ears.

"What is it?" asked Enzo.

"I'm going to report you to the bureau of hygiene!"

"What for?"

"Because this plate stinks!"

"That's impossible!"

"I'm telling you it stinks so bad you can smell it a mile away! Can you tell me what was on it before?"

"How should I know? After they're washed, the dishes are all the same! They're clean!"

"I'll tell you what was on it before! You don't have to

be a fortune-teller to know! You just have to have a nose! It was fish!"

"Cavalié, you—"

The other cut him off.

"How do you wash them, by hand or in a dish-washer?"

"In a dishwasher."

"And you trust a dishwasher? Big mistake! Whenever you pick up a washed dish, you must check to see if it's actually clean! Because there might still be a trace of what there was before!"

He didn't calm down until after he'd sniffed for a long time the new dish Enzo had brought him. The owner had washed it by hand and finished drying it before their eyes.

Montalbano ate without much conviction and then left the restaurant in a hurry because the cavaliere had started making another fuss.

Sitting down on the flat rock to smoke a cigarette, he started thinking that rarely, during his life as a cop, had he ever found himself so hard up for ideas as now.

Better just distract himself by teasing the usual crab or recalling the scene Cavaliere Jocolano had made . . .

Wait a second, Montalbà.

Stop right there.

Something passed through your head for a second while the cavaliere was talking, something that lit up like a match in the night and then immediately went out.

What was it?

He tried to remember.

The flash in his brain was so bright and sudden that he gave a start.

"Can you tell me what was on it before?"

No, he couldn't.

He hadn't even asked himself the question.

He went immediately back to the office.

"Fazio! We're a couple of imbeciles!"

"Why do you say that?"

"What was in the two warehouses that the bombs were placed in front of?"

"Nothing, Chief. They were empty."

"Because they'd been put in the dishwasher."

Fazio looked at him as if he'd gone mad.

"The warehouses? In the dishwasher?!"

"Never mind that. But before they were empty, they must have had something inside them, mustn't they?"

"Of course."

"And do you know what?"

"No, I don't."

"Find out at once."

"But do you really think it's so important?"

"I can't really say."

"All it takes is a phone call," said Fazio, leaving the room.

Five minutes later he was back. Before saying anything, he looked at Montalbano with admiration.

"How did you figure it out?"

"Never mind," the inspector repeated. "Just tell me."

"The two warehouses held computers, printers, ink cartridges . . ."

"Ah," said Montalbano.

"And the same person who first rented the one on Via Pisacane later moved into the warehouse on Via Palermo, because the first one was too small."

"Do you know this person's name?"

"Yessir, I do." Fazio's eyes were sparkling. "Lombardo. Adriano Lombardo."

"Liliana's husband?"

"Yessir."

They looked at each other in puzzlement. Montalbano recovered quickly.

"Wait a second, wait just one second. This means that the bombs were intended for Lombardo. That they were warnings that only he could understand. Right?"

"Right."

"So now I ask: Why didn't they put the bomb in the warehouse he currently uses, whose address we don't know, where he most certainly keeps his merchandise?"

"Because maybe he never rented a third warehouse."

"So where's he keeping the computers, then?"

"Probably in Marinella, at home. Maybe that's why he often goes there."

The inspector's reply was immediate.

"Aside from the fact that they could have planted a bomb at the house, and didn't, I don't think all of Lombardo's stuff could fit in the only extra room they have."

Fazio said nothing.

"Here we must make a conjecture," the inspector resumed. "Which is that Lombardo transferred his stuff to some town nearby, and his enemies don't know where."

"That's possible," said Fazio.

"And the reason for the bombs might be failure to pay the protection racket."

Fazio seemed doubtful.

"Not convinced?"

"No. Because they planted the bombs not when Lombardo's stuff was inside, but after the places had been emptied out. It doesn't make any sense. Especially if Lombardo didn't rent any other warehouse space in Vigàta and isn't keeping his merchandise at his house."

He had a point.

"Let's try to catch Lombardo and ask him to explain," Fazio suggested.

Montalbano shook his head.

"The guy'll laugh in our faces. He'll say the bombs had nothing to do with him and he knows nothing about them."

"So what can we do?"

"Liliana must certainly know the whole story. We

should talk to her, but at the moment I'm the least suitable person for the job."

Without warning he slapped himself in the forehead.

"Why didn't I think of that sooner?"

"Think of what sooner?"

"Of sending Mimì Augello to buy himself a suit in Montelusa. Go and get him immediately."

Fazio left and came back with Augello.

"Mimì, when was the last time you bought yourself a new suit?"

"About a year ago. Why?"

"I'll explain later. Do you know a big store in Montelusa called All'ultima moda?"

"Yeah, I've been there with my wife."

"Sorry to ask a personal question, but how long does it take you, normally, to win a woman's confidence?"

"I can see you haven't got much experience in these matters. The amount of time is rather variable. A lot depends on the woman."

"Would one morning suffice?"

"Alone, one on one?"

"No, with others around."

Mimì didn't open his mouth.

"Well?"

"I'm not going to tell you unless you tell me first what you're cooking up."

Montalbano told him.

The light was on in the Lombardo home, but there was no sign of Liliana. He was putting the key in the lock when he heard the telephone ring. This time he got to it in time, managing to pick up the receiver right in the middle of a ring.

"Hello?"

There was definitely someone at the other end, but whoever it was, they remained silent.

"Hello?"

They hung up.

He went and opened the refrigerator. Adelina had made *sartù di riso alla calabrisa* and swordfish *involtini*. He prepared himself for a pleasant evening.

After he lit the oven to warm up the dishes, the telephone rang again.

"Hello?"

"It's Liliana."

11

He wasn't all that surprised. The situation between them remained all too confused, not to mention that he'd left her in the lurch. Sooner or later she was going to demand an explanation.

Since Liliana hadn't said anything else, the inspector spoke.

"Did you call just a few minutes ago?" he asked.

"Yes, I heard your car drive by, and I couldn't . . ."

She fell silent again. Was she going to say "resist"? The intonation she'd given to her sentence seemed to suggest this.

"Why did you hang up?"

"I don't know."

If they'd been at the station, he would have continued: And why are you calling me now?

But he remained silent. As did Liliana. After a few

moments, she broke the ice, though she still seemed un-comfortable.

"Will you believe me if I say I can hardly remember anything that happened last night?"

Let her talk, Montalbà; don't you dare open your mouth.

"I drank too much," she continued, "and must have said some . . . well, inappropriate things, to make you run away like that. I want to thank you."

"For what?"

"For not . . . taking advantage of me."

She was good, no doubt about it. She'd turned the tables and passed the hot potato to him with nonchalance and elegance. Now it was his turn, and he had to be careful what he said.

"I ran away because I was needed at the office."

"Duty always first, eh?"

Was she being ironic?

"Well, that sets my mind at rest. So it wasn't that I made you feel uneasy," she concluded.

There was another pause. The inspector now wanted her to lay down the first card.

"I want to talk to you," said Liliana.

She clearly wanted to start the whole business all over again.

So the inspector decided to shake things up a little. It was a good way, and a good moment, to find out what sort of relationship she really had with her husband, a man who appeared and disappeared at will, and about whom nobody knew anything.

"Speaking of which," he said, "could you tell me where your husband is at the moment?"

"Adriano?!" asked Liliana, taken aback.

"Why, do you have another husband with a different name?"

She was too overwhelmed by the inspector's first question to react to his quip.

"What is this? Why do you want to know?"

She seemed seriously concerned; her tone was apprehensive. Montalbano improvised:

"Somebody's filed charges against him for a brawl he was apparently involved in a few days ago."

"Are you sure they mean Adriano?"

"That's precisely why I want to talk to him."

Liliana hesitated before responding.

"Look, I honestly don't know where he is at the moment. But if you want, I can call him right now and have him ring you at home."

It was clear she didn't want to give him her husband's telephone number. This was in fact where Montalbano wanted to go with this. Why was Adriano Lombardo so guarded?

"It's not really all that urgent. And actually, you could give me a hand yourself."

"How?"

"I'll repeat the basic facts of the accusation to you. Adriano Lombardo, son of Giovanni Lombardo and Nicoletta Valenza—"

"No!" Liliana interrupted him. "That's wrong! Adriano's father's name was Stefano and he died seven years ago, and his mother's maiden name was Maria Donati."

"So much the better. A case of mistaken identity, apparently. I guess that settles that."

"Well, I'm glad. And what's the plan for us?"

He played dumb.

"In what sense?"

"When will we see each other again?"

Pushy, the lady.

"Look, tonight I can't do anything. I'm waiting for some phone calls to do with work."

"So when, then?"

"Are you going to work tomorrow?"

"Of course."

"You haven't got your car back yet, have you?"

"No."

"Then I'll see you tomorrow morning at eight, and we'll decide on a time and place. Okay?"

"Well, if there's no other way . . . then okay," she said.

She was disappointed, and she'd let him know.

He hung up.

And so, thought the inspector, tomorrow I shall

do my part to have you meet my second in command, Inspector Mimì Augello, a man who could teach Don Juan a thing or two.

He set the table on the veranda and contentedly ate the sartù, the involtini, and a big dish of chicory so bitter it seemed poisonous. Then he sat down in an armchair to watch some TV.

Ragonese was careful not to talk about what had happened to him. This time he laid into the mayor and the garbage problem.

A little later Livia rang. She seemed to be in a good mood.

"I had some fun today."

"Where'd you go?"

"I'm not going to tell you."

"Then you'll make me suspect the worst."

"Please, Inspector, don't suspect."

"Then tell me where you've been."

"A friend of mine dragged me to a fortune-teller."

Montalbano lit up like a match.

"What's this nonsense? So now you're going to fortune-tellers? Pretty soon it'll be wizards and witches!"

"Come on, Salvo . . ."

"Come on, my eye! I certainly hope you didn't believe what the lady told you!"

"So I shouldn't believe it?"

"Absolutely not! You would be a fool to believe it!"

"Too bad."

"Why too bad?"

"Because she assured me that you were very faithful to me."

He'd fallen straight into the trap, which enraged him even more. A blowout was inevitable.

———

Liliana was waiting for him at the gate. She got in the car but didn't kiss him. She merely said:

"Ciao, Salvo."

She wasn't as cheerful as all the other times, and all she did during the drive was stare at the road. It didn't fit with the way she'd acted on the phone the previous evening. It was possible she'd received some news during the night, or early that morning, which had upset her.

They'd agreed that during their morning drive they would decide on where and when to meet next, but she didn't mention it. And Montalbano didn't bring it up, either.

Before getting out at the bus stop, she turned to Montalbano and said she would phone him in the evening.

"Ciao."

And that was that. No kiss, no caresses. Her mind was clearly elsewhere.

———

The first part of the morning went smoothly. Then, just before noon, Catarella called him to tell him that Tommaseo, the public prosecutor, was on the line.

"Hello, sir; what can I do for you?"

"I received your report denouncing that journalist . . . what's his name . . ."

"Ragonese."

"Right. And I've had a . . . ch . . . chance to . . . l . . . look . . . at the . . . the v . . . vid . . . eo . . ."

The prosecutor stopped, unable to go any further. He was out of breath.

The stammering fit had been brought on by the sight of a half-naked Liliana on the bed.

Prosecutor Tommaseo, who was known not to have a woman in his life, was a proper sex maniac who never actually had sex and therefore drooled after every pretty woman he saw, dead or alive.

"What do you think?"

"Stu . . . pen . . . dous . . . !"

"I didn't mean the lady, sir, but my report. Do you think you'll act on it right away?"

"Do . . . re . . . re . . . mi . . . mind . . . m . . . me . . . f . . . fa . . . first . . . so l . . . so . . . little time . . ."

Would he manage to sing the whole scale?

"A la . . . la . . . lot . . . t . . . t . . . to . . . do . . ."

Yes!

"Do you plan to call her in for questioning?"

"One . . . one . . . too . . . too many . . . things to do. Th . . . three days . . ."

Good God, was he going to start counting now? Up to what? A hundred? A thousand? At this rate they'd be there till nightfall. Montalbano hung up. If the guy called back, he'd tell him they got cut off. But Tommaseo never called back.

Instead a call came in from Mimì Augello.

"So you didn't go to Montelusa?"

"Of course I did! I'm calling from right outside the store."

"And so?

"Listen, Salvo, when I got here it must have been around nine thirty, and I combed all three floors of the store without ever seeing the lady you described to me."

"Maybe you didn't see her because she was back in a dressing room with a customer who was trying on some clothes."

"Don't you think I thought of that myself? And so I stood outside the line of dressing rooms and waited. Nothing, no sign of her. And so I went up to a salesgirl and struck up a conversation, saying I was the husband of a customer. At a certain point I asked her about Signora Lombardo, and she told me her boss had come in on time, but five minutes later she'd got a call on her cell phone that seemed to upset her, after which she said she was taking a day of sick leave and left. So I called to tell you this. But now I have to go because the store's about to close for lunch."

"What do you care if the store's about to close?"

"Salvo, just think for a second. I couldn't very well let

the whole morning go to waste. I'm taking the salesgirl out to lunch. Her name's Lucia and I assure you she's—"

Montalbano hung up.

What the hell was happening to Liliana? Was something amiss?

Leaving the office to go to Enzo's, he asked Catarella if he had any news of Fazio, whom he hadn't seen all morning.

"'E called at eight this mornin', Chief, sayin' as how 'e was gonna betoken hisself to Montelusa."

"Did he say what he was going to do there?"

"Nah, Chief, 'e din't."

As soon as he got in his car, the inspector changed his mind and headed for Marinella. It was possible Liliana had gone home. Driving past her house, he slowed down. The gate and windows were closed. She wasn't home, or at least was pretending she wasn't. He turned around and went off to eat.

He'd already finished when Enzo came up to him and said he was wanted on the phone.

It was Mimì Augello.

"Sorry, Salvo, but since Lucia—"

"Who's Lucia?"

"The salesgirl. I'm having lunch with her . . . By the way, I told my wife, Beba, that I have to go on a stakeout tonight, so please, don't pull any of your usual stunts . . ."

"Fine, but what was it you wanted to tell me?"

"I don't know if it's of any importance . . . You told me this Liliana had something going with a young salesman, Arturo Tallarita, right?"

"Right."

"Well, Lucia, who talks a lot, told me that Tallarita didn't come into work this morning. And he didn't call to say he wouldn't be coming."

"Thanks, Mimì."

"But I mean it about Beba. If she happens to call, be sure to confirm that I have to stay out tonight for work."

Want to bet the two lovers fled in secret on an amorous escapade? Just like Mimì was getting ready to do? Maybe even for only a day, to be spent in total freedom, without having to hide anything from anybody . . .

———

"What did you go to Montelusa for?"

"I spent the morning at the Chamber of Commerce."

"Why?"

"I wanted some information on Adriano Lombardo. And I hoped to find out whether he had a warehouse in some other town in the province."

"Discover anything interesting?"

"Nothing. Or, actually, I found out that he'd given first the warehouse on Via Pisacane as his business address, then the one on Via Palermo. And after that, he wrote that he'd abandoned the one on Via Palermo too, and his new business address was in Marinella."

"So we're back to the hypothesis that we already sort of formulated, which is that if he rented a third warehouse, it must be in some town outside the province."

"Exactly. You want me to keep looking?"

"Yes, but in your spare time."

"Any news of Inspector Augello?"

"Yes."

"Good news?"

"For him, yes. For us, no."

"What's that mean?"

Montalbano explained.

In the end Fazio stared at him skeptically.

"You really think Liliana and Arturo ran away together?"

"Don't you?"

"I have my doubts."

"Explain."

"Disappearing from their workplace for a whole day will have everyone thinking that there's something going on between them, or at least some kind of arrangement. They're actually doing the exact opposite of what they'd been doing so carefully up until the day before."

The argument made sense.

"And so?"

"Maybe they were forced."

"By whom?"

"You know what I say, Chief? Let's just wait and see.

Oh, and I almost forgot. Give me the keys to the car you're driving."

"Why?"

"So I can take it back to the body shop and pick up yours, which is ready."

He gave him the keys.

Then something occurred to him.

"Would you do me a favor?"

"Anytime, Chief."

"Could you go right now and pay a call on Signora Tallarita?"

"Sure. What do you want to know?"

"If she has any news of her son."

"All right."

"But don't let on about anything; I don't want to alarm her. I'll wait for you here."

———

Fazio returned about an hour later.

"Chief, there wasn't any need to take precautions. Signora Tallarita was already pretty upset on her own. So upset, in fact, that when I told her who I was, she almost fainted."

"What was wrong?"

"She hasn't heard from Arturo since last night. He went out after dinner, telling his mother he'd be back late. But he never returned. Then this morning she got a phone call from someone at the clothing store wanting to know why her son hadn't come in to work. And the call got her pretty upset."

"And what did you tell her?"

"That if she wanted to report him missing, I was at her disposal. But she refused."

Fazio paused, then continued.

"Chief, I have the impression she knows about her son's affair with Signora Liliana."

"Oh, really?"

"She started muttering to herself about some big slut—those were her exact words—and then, under her breath, said something about Marinella, or so it seemed to me . . ."

"How could she have known?"

"Probably the guy who lends his Volvo to Arturo— the neighbor, Miccichè."

It seemed a fair bet.

"I'll go now and get the car."

Unexpectedly, Augello showed up.

"Did Lucia stand you up?"

"Are you kidding? We've got a date at eight thirty. I wanted to tell you something. After I called you at the restaurant, Lucia started talking again about La Lombardo. She said that Liliana was really upset after she got that phone call. And when the manager didn't want to give her the day off, she made a big scene."

When it was time, Montalbano went out of his office, grabbed the keys that Fazio had left with Catarella, and went out to the parking lot. When he saw his car there, he stopped to look at it. Todaro had done an excellent job.

He drove off towards Marinella.

And the whole way there he never stopped wondering why Arturo and Liliana had disappeared.

Arturo had left first, then Liliana. The person who called her at the store was probably Arturo himself.

Maybe to warn her about some new and dangerous development.

Montalbano was driving so slowly that when he had to stop before turning into the driveway, his engine stalled.

He started it back up but botched the maneuver as the car lurched forward through the air and then stalled again, spanning the road crosswise.

A pandemonium of horn blasts and insults ensued.

Montalbano didn't even hear them.

He just sat there, immobile, hands on the steering wheel, goggle-eyed.

He'd remembered.

It was right here, in this very spot, that the shot had been fired at his car, when he'd made the same driving mistake the evening when he was returning with Liliana after eating arancini at Adelina's house.

And he'd mistaken the sound of the shot against the body of the car for a stone bouncing up.

At last he successfully made the maneuver and turned onto the narrow lane.

Total darkness reigned in the Lombardo house.

His appetite was gone. Grabbing a bottle of whisky and a glass, he went and sat outside on the veranda.

They had shot to kill.

They had aimed correctly.

They hadn't counted, however, on the car suddenly lurching forward and up.

And they had no intention of shooting him. If it was him they had wanted to kill, the man with the rifle would have to have been on the other side of the road.

Therefore, they'd tried to eliminate Liliana.

There could be no doubt about this.

12

The revelation had a rather curious effect on the inspector. The shock, incredulity, and bewilderment were very short-lived, all things considered, because immediately, like an air bubble released by the stone that had kept it long imprisoned at the bottom of the sea, a full awareness, an absolute certainty rose to the surface of his mind: namely, the fact that he had always suspected Liliana not only of not being what she seemed to be, but also of hiding within herself the answers to almost all the questions that had been besieging him over the past few days.

At any rate, the confirmation he'd just had gave him a different perspective on everything that had happened until then.

He now had to reexamine the whole picture from the start, from a different perspective.

Because it was no longer a case of little white lies,

shows put on for the viewing public, and lost scoops, but of attempted murder.

The qualitative leap was considerable. It dispelled the playful atmosphere that had characterized his relationship with Liliana.

It was possible that by getting others to think she was his girlfriend, she was seeking help, or protection.

But how should he now proceed?

Should he wait for Liliana to come back home, which she was bound to do sooner or later? Or should he go out looking for her? And what would he say once he found her?

Should he interrogate her? And on the basis of what concrete facts?

He needed help. There was no point in asking Mimì, at least not that night. He rang Fazio.

"Sorry to call so late. Have you finished eating?"

"Just now."

"Feel up to coming over to my place?"

"I'm on my way."

Twenty minutes later, Fazio was knocking at the door. He'd come running. No doubt his curiosity was eating him alive.

"Did you notice if the lights were on at the Lombardos'?"

"No, it was all dark."

Montalbano sat him down on the veranda and told him what he'd just remembered.

Fazio seemed disturbed by it all, but his wisdom gained the upper hand.

"Chief, my conclusion is that it's not clear they wanted to kill her for any direct involvement in anything. It might be they wanted to take revenge for some offense committed by one of her men, Arturo or her husband. A proxy vendetta."

"That's possible. But it's clear that she's the one we should be working on."

"What do you think you'll do?" Fazio asked with a dark expression on his face.

"I called you here because two heads are better than one. In my opinion, the first thing we should do is find Liliana."

"I agree."

"But how? She's probably with Arturo, but we don't really know."

"We could check all the hotels in the province."

"We might just be wasting our time."

"What if we sent out an all-points bulletin to all the stations on the island?"

"I think that'd be another waste of time. No, we need to track her down right away. If they tried to get her once, you can be sure they'll try again."

As the inspector was saying these words, something suddenly occurred to him.

"What is it?" asked Fazio.

Montalbano looked puzzled.

"I didn't say anything!"

"Chief, I've known you too long not to be able to tell when you get a new idea. What were you thinking?"

"I was thinking that it's quite possible that at this very moment, Liliana and Arturo are just a hop, skip, and a jump away from us, holed up in her house, sitting in the dark so that everyone will think there's nobody there."

"Yeah, but if we go and knock on the door, they won't answer."

"Who said anything about knocking on the door?"

Fazio understood at once.

"Be sure to wear gloves," he said.

"Don't make me laugh! My fingerprints are all over the house already, by the hundreds! Do you know how many things I must have touched the night I had dinner there? You're the one who should wear gloves!"

To open the door Montalbano used a set of jimmies an old burglar had once given him. It took him very little time, and he didn't make a sound. Fazio came in behind him.

As soon as they were inside, Montalbano sniffed the air. He could still smell the morning coffee. He pricked up his ears.

There wasn't a sound. It was so quiet, in fact, that they should have been able to hear someone breathing.

"There's nobody here," Fazio said softly.

"Turn on the flashlight."

The place looked pretty messy. The first door on the right led to the bedroom. And that room was really messy. The armoire was thrown wide open, and clearly some clothes were missing. Panties and bras were scattered across the floor and the bed.

"Liliana," the inspector said, "must have come back here, packed a suitcase, and left."

"So we can leave, too," said Fazio, who didn't like these little adventures of his boss's.

"Lemme just see something first. Light my way."

They went to the house's extra room. The door was locked, but the inspector opened it with a picklock. There was a single bed and a small armoire inside. On a metal shelf were five computers and four printers.

"It's too small for storage. He doesn't keep his computers here," said Fazio.

They went out, and the inspector relocked the door behind him.

They went back to the veranda and sat down.

"If nothing else," said Montalbano, "we now know that Liliana has fled. And that it won't be a brief absence of a day or two, but much longer. In fact it's anybody's guess when we'll see her again."

"After getting the phone call at work," said Fazio, "she must have come back here on the bus, packed her bags, and cut out. But how? She couldn't have set out on foot with a suitcase in her hand. So did she take some sort of public transportation? A taxi or a bus? And if she took a bus, which one did she take? There are so many that pass on the provincial road—to Montereale, to Fiacca, to Trapani, to Palermo, to Catania . . ."

"We're going to have to look into it."

"I'll take care of it, starting early tomorrow morning."

There was no point in keeping Fazio any longer. The inspector saw him to the door and said good-bye.

Later, besieged by worries as he was, it took the hand of God to make him fall asleep.

At ten past seven, as he was about to leave the house, he got a phone call from Fazio.

"I talked to the taxi services. She didn't call any. I can try the bus offices, but it'll take too long."

"Never mind. I'll be coming to the office a little later, around eight thirty, nine. Wait for me."

He set off like a rocket for Vigàta, but instead of going to the station, he headed for Via Pisacane.

Five minutes later he was knocking at Signora Tallarita's door. As soon as the inspector saw her, he felt sorry for her. It was clear the poor woman was devastated and had been up all night, probably crying most of the time.

She recognized Montalbano at once.

"What's happened to Arturo?"

She grabbed his arms and clung to them.

"We know even less than you, signora."

The woman let go of him and started crying again.

"He's never done this before, going off for so long without saying anything! He's changed! Ever since he met that slut . . ."

She stopped and stole a glance at the inspector to see how he reacted to what had just slipped out of her mouth. Montalbano decided to lay his cards on the table. He didn't have any time to waste beating around the bush.

"Are you referring to Liliana Lombardo?"

The signora's eyes opened wide.

"How do you know about her?"

"*Cara signora,* we know everything," Montalbano said in a tone worse than if he'd been the head of the CIA. "We've had an eye on her for a while."

"The tramp! The hussy!" Signora Tallarita exploded.

"Now, signora, I want you to answer some questions for me. In your son, Arturo's, interest."

"You think he ran away with her?"

"It's one of the possible scenarios."

"All right, go ahead and ask."

"You heard about the relations between Arturo and Signora Lombardo from your neighbor Miccichè, correct?"

Signora Tallarita gave him a puzzled look.

"Miccichè? What's that poor man have to do with any of this? The guy's already embalmed and in a casket!"

She was being sincere, clearly. Montalbano, too, felt

puzzled. He was convinced that the person who'd told her about it was Miccichè, but he didn't let it show.

"So who was it, then?"

"One day, in the stairwell, I ran into Signor Nicotra . . ."

"Carlo Nicotra?"

"Him. And he tol' me everything and said the whole town was talking about it and saying terrible things and that this woman was a bad one, and that she would ruin my son."

She started crying uncontrollably again, as Montalbano was having trouble digesting her answer.

"Signora, one last question and I'll stop bothering you. Do you know Signora Lombardo's cell phone number?"

"N . . . no."

It wasn't true. The woman didn't know how to lie.

"Signora, the more you hide the truth, the less chance there is for us to locate Arturo."

This convinced her.

"All right, I know it."

"Have you ever called Signora Lombardo?"

"Yes."

"When?"

"Yesterday morning, when I saw that my son had spent the night out and hadn't come home yet, I got worried; I started looking through his things and I found a little book with a lot of phone numbers in it."

"And so you called her?"

"Yessir."

"What time was it, more or less?"

"It was probably around nine in the morning."

"And what did you say to her?"

"I asked her if my son had spent the night with her."

"And what did she say?"

"She said no and hung up. The whore! The stinking slut! If I ever get my hands on her I'll wring her neck like a chicken's!"

When she'd calmed down a little, the inspector thanked her, promised he would keep her informed, and headed for the door.

Signora Tallarita wanted to see him out. Which meant that Montalbano was forced to go down one flight of stairs, wait a few minutes, then come back up on tiptoe.

This time he knocked on Miccichè's door.

A woman wearing a small hat and pushing a tiny shopping cart came to the door.

"Whattayou want? I'm going out."

"I'm Inspector Montalbano, police."

He'd spoken softly, worried that Signora Tallarita might hear him.

"Wha'??" said the woman. "Talk louder, I can't hear too good."

"I can't. I have a hoarse voice."

Meanwhile Miccichè himself arrived in his wheel-chair.

"Please come in, come in."

The woman went out, grumbling about people wasting her time. The inspector went inside, closing the door behind him.

"I'll just take up a minute of your time. Do you know whether Arturo took your Volvo last night?"

Miccichè made a worried face.

"Did something happen?"

"Arturo hasn't been heard from. So, did he take the car?"

"I don't know."

"Do you have copies of the keys to the garage?"

"Yes."

"Let me have them, I'll bring them right back."

Miccichè handed them to him.

"It's number eleven, right?"

"Yes."

The Volvo was there, in the garage. The engine was cold. It hadn't been driven for several days. Which wasn't a very good sign.

He brought the keys back to Miccichè, who seemed pleased to know that his car had nothing to do with Arturo's disappearance.

———

The only hope was to try another hypothesis. Montalbano went to the mechanic's.

"So, when's Signora Lombardo's car going to be ready?"

The mechanic gave him an embarrassed look.

"What, you mean the lady didn't tell you, Inspector?"

"Tell me what?"

"Yesterday morning, around nine thirty, she called me to ask if the car was ready. I said I could have it ready by noon. And so she asked me if I could bring it to her house."

"And did you?"

"Of course. She paid, and that was the end of that."

"Was she alone?"

"She was alone. But I didn't go inside the house."

"Do me a favor. Give me the model and the license number."

The mechanic gave him the information without any comment.

⬛

"So," said Fazio, "she escaped in her own car. Maybe with Arturo."

"I doubt it," said Montalbano.

"Why?"

"When I drove Liliana into town yesterday morning, she was very nervous. I thought maybe she'd had a fight with Arturo. Whereas I now think she was nervous because she hadn't heard from him. And when Signora Tallarita phoned her at the store, it confirmed her fear that Arturo had disappeared. Which threw her into a panic, to the point where she picked up her car and drove away. All of which means that the two of them knew they were playing with fire."

"But where could she have gone?"

"I have a vague idea. But if I tell you, I'm afraid Mr. C'mishner's gonna want me to take that test again."

Fazio gave a start.

"What test?"

"The mental health check."

Fazio's eyes opened even wider.

"When did you take it?"

"Don't worry, it was only a dream I had."

Fazio breathed a sigh of relief.

"Just tell me your idea. I'm not the commissioner."

"In my opinion, Liliana ran to her husband."

"Why do you say that?"

"You once said to me that Liliana and Arturo might have an arrangement and that the kid probably knew about the whole song and dance Liliana was acting out with me. So what if Liliana became Arturo's lover based on an agreement she made with her husband? Or better yet, on her husband's orders?"

Fazio thought about this for a minute.

"For what purpose?"

"I don't know yet."

"But if that was the case, where would it lead us?" Fazio asked.

"The answer is easy: either into a dead end or onto a superhighway leading straight to the truth."

"We absolutely have to find Lombardo," said Fazio. "Without wasting another minute."

"Right. Speaking of which, didn't you tell me Carlo Nicotra had no interest in Arturo?"

"Yes, I did."

"Then you should know that the person who put the bee in Mamma Tallarita's bonnet by portraying Liliana as a danger to her son was none other than Carlo Nicotra."

"Really?!"

"Really. In short, maybe Nicotra's not gay, but he certainly wants Arturo all to himself."

"Chief, if that's the way it is, it's not because Nicotra's in love with Arturo, but because the whole thing's got something to do with drugs. I would bet the house on it."

"And I *will* bet the house on it. Let me ask you a question. Isn't it possible that Arturo replaced his father, who's in jail? And that's why Nicotra's keeping tabs on him?"

Fazio looked doubtful.

"But where's the kid gonna find the time to deal drugs? Unless Arturo's dealing right out of the store where he works . . ."

"He might be. Why don't you mosey up to Montelusa and pay a call on your friend in Narcotics? Those guys usually know where the prime dealing spots are."

"I'll go right now," said Fazio, getting up.

"Wait," said Montalbano.

Fazio sat back down.

This time the idea Montalbano had in mind was too

crazy even to be expressed. He decided to try to find out what he wanted to know by making something up on the spot.

"It just occurred to me that while you're in Montelusa, I could try to track down Lombardo."

"By calling all the police commissariats?"

"I repeat, it would only be a waste of time. If anything concrete had happened, that would be a different story."

"So how are you going to do it?"

"It's possible the central management of the company Lombardo works for is informed of his moves."

"Good idea."

"What's the company called?"

"Star Computer. Its headquarters is in Milan. Want me to look up the address?"

"No, that's all right. I can do it myself."

It wasn't the sort of thing to get Catarella involved in; the guy was liable to stir up pandemonium from here to Timbuktu. He summoned Gallo instead.

"Shut the door and sit down."

"Yessir, Chief."

"I want you to call Information, using my outside line here, and ask for the telephone number of the Star Computer firm in Milan."

Gallo got it right away and wrote it down on a sheet of paper.

"Now call the company's switchboard, tell them you're the secretary of the Honorable Rizzopinna of the Anti-Mafia Commission, and you want to talk to the chief of personnel."

"And then what?"

"When the chief of personnel comes to the phone, you say: 'Please hold, I'll put the Honorable Rizzopinna on the line.' And turn on the speakerphone."

13

It all went off without a hitch. Montalbano had time to review the multiplication tables for seven before a decisive voice, the kind used to giving orders, asked:

"Hello? Who is this?"

More than a question, it was a command, a sort of "Identify yourself!" By way of reply, Montalbano assumed the tone of someone who considers talking with common mortals a waste of time and therefore skimps on the pauses between words.

"IbelieveyouwerealreadytoldI'mtheHonorableOrazio RizzopinnadiCastelbuono,auxiliarymemberoftheNational-ParliamentaryCommissionforSubordinateLabor."

He'd forgotten he was on the Anti-Mafia Commission. But he knew from experience that long and complicated names and titles always had an effect.

Indeed the voice at the other end immediately lost all its authority.

"Good morning, sir; what can I do for you?"

"CouldyoupleasetellmewithwhomIamspeaking?"

"Gianni Brambilla, chief of personnel."

"Ah,finally!Ineedsomeinformation."

"I'm at your service."

"Arethesoleagentsofthecompanyundertheauthority ofyouroffice?"

"Of course."

"Couldyoutellmeifamannamed . . . justasec ond . . .hereweare . . .ifamannamedAdrianoLombardo, that'stheone,isstillyoursolelicensedrepresentativeforall ofSicily?"

"Sir, could you please hold the line for a minute?"

"Yes,butpleasebequickaboutit."

Gallo stared at the inspector in wonder.

Brambilla was back in a jiffy.

"Here we are, sir. Lombardo was let go three months ago. He is no longer our representative. Insufficient returns. He has given back his stocks of merchandise."

"Thankyou."

Just as he had thought. His idea hadn't been so crazy after all.

"Still need me, Chief?" asked Gallo.

"No, thanks. And remember, don't tell Catarella what I had you do, otherwise he'll feel bad."

As soon as Gallo left, the inspector sent for Augello.

"How'd it go with the salesgirl?"

"It was part fun and part not."

"Why not?"

"Jesus, does that girl like to talk! She won't shut up for even a second; she's capable of blabbing even when she's . . ."

Montalbano preferred not to listen to the details.

"Oh, yeah? And while she was doing all this blabbing, did she happen to tell you that Arturo Tallarita is a drug dealer?"

"No, she didn't mention anything like that. Not even remotely. I now know every detail about the life of every person who works in that store from the time they were born. So I'm pretty sure that if he was a dealer, she would have told me."

"Are you aware that Arturo and La Lombardo have vanished?"

Augello didn't bat an eyelash.

"Did they run away together?"

"I really don't think so."

"Then what's going on?"

Montalbano told him the whole story, from the attempted murder of Liliana to the latest discovery that Adriano Lombardo had been sacked from his company.

"That last fact might also not mean anything," said Mimì. "He might have got a better offer from the competition and accepted."

And this, too, might be true. But then why did Liliana say he was still a sales representative and why was he still spinning around Sicily like a top?

"Well, how would you go about tracking him down?"

"Lombardo? That's easier said than done. By now it's possible he's no longer even in Sicily."

"But what if he was?"

"Well, you get all the police commissariats—"

"You and Fazio are fixated on this idea of the police commissariats! You know how they deal with requests like this! If there isn't a really good reason for it, they don't take it seriously. It would take them a month to get back to us, if they got back to us at all."

"So give it a good reason, then."

"What am I gonna do, write that he's wanted for murder?"

"You needn't go so far."

"Give me an example."

"Well, you could say that his wife, whom we're investigating—which is perfectly true since someone has made an attempt on her life—has disappeared without a trace and we therefore absolutely have to get in touch with her husband."

He was right.

"Okay, Mimì, do me a favor. You handle it."

"All right."

Fazio returned about an hour later.

"Narcotics has no indication whatsoever that anybody's dealing drugs out of that store."

Montalbano told him the latest news.

"So all we can do now is wait," said Fazio, resigned.

But by this point the inspector could feel his blood simmering and had no desire to sit still any longer.

He had another idea.

As Fazio looked on with an inquisitive expression on his face, Montalbano grabbed the telephone and called Adelina. Who immediately became alarmed.

"Wha', you didna like what I cook a lest night?"

"It was excellent. I just need to ask you something."

"Wha' you wanna know?"

"Okay, listen carefully, Adelì. You remember Signora Lombardo, the lady who came with me to your place to eat arancini . . . ?"

"Sure! How could I forget?"

"Do you know by any chance whether she has a cleaning woman who comes on a regular basis to her house?"

"Yeah, she does."

"Do you know her?"

"Yessah, I do. She take a same a bus to Marinella as a me, tree times a week."

"Do you know her name?"

"Concetta Altellia."

"Do you know where she lives?"

"Sure I do. Close to me. Vicolo Gesù e Maria, bu' I dunno the number."

"Thanks, Adelì."

He rang Catarella on the internal line.

"Cat, I want you to look up a number for me in the phone book. See if you can find anything under the name of . . . wait . . . Altellia."

Catarella remained silent at his end, but the inspector could hear him breathing.

"Cat, what are you doing?"

"I'm awaitin', Chief."

"For what?"

"For the poisson's name."

"What person?"

"The poisson whoseabouts you said 'Wait an' I'll tell ya.'"

"Cat, that's the person's name: Altellia. Just as your name is Catarella, this person's name is Altellia. Got that?"

"Yeah, now I got it, Chief."

Moments later Catarella's voice came on again.

"I can't fine no Altellia inna drecktory. But I foun' Altellini. Whaddo I do, Chief, call 'im?"

After all, for Catarella, one name was as good as another.

"No."

"You know what I'm gonna do?" Montalbano said to Fazio as he set down the receiver. "After lunch I'm gonna go and pay her a visit myself. Actually, you should come too. We'll meet at Enzo's in an hour and a half."

At lunch he made sure to eat lightly, to keep his head as clear as possible.

Fazio was on time. They got in the car and drove off to Vicolo Gesù e Maria. Luckily the little street consisted of three small three-story apartment buildings on either side. This was a stroke of luck they hadn't expected.

Naturally the first building entrance they came to had no intercom system. But it was open. They went into the courtyard and noticed a man to their left, sitting on a wicker chair and smoking a pipe.

They went up to him. He must have mixed dog shit in with the tobacco he was smoking, because the air around him stank. Even the flies were keeping their distance.

"Excuse me, could you tell us whether Concetta Altellia . . ." Fazio began.

"She's my daughter."

"Could you tell your daughter—"

"I don' talk to her no more an' I don' wanna talk to her no more. We live together, bu' we don' talk. We had a fight. The bitch don' wan' me to smoke my pipe in the house."

And he spat, missing Fazio's shoe by about a millimeter with a clot of dense brown material that looked like prune jam.

You really couldn't blame the daughter.

"Then tell me please what floor you live on."

"Seccon' floor. Seccon' door to the right."

"Is she at home?"

"If she warn't, whattayou think? You think I'd be smokin' ousside?"

Concetta Altellia was fat and about fifty, with a face that let you know straight off that she never backed down from a fight. In fact she probably never let a minute go by without starting a row with someone.

"Whattaya want?"

"I'm Inspector Montalbano, police, and this is Inspector Fazio."

"I didna ask who you was, but what you want."

"We want to talk to you."

"An' whattaya think, that I got time to waste talkin' to youse?"

The inspector looked at Fazio, who then intervened.

"All right then, you'll have to come down to the station with us."

"Are you fuckin' kiddin' me?"

"Either you let us in, or we'll run you in," Fazio replied in all seriousness, and then, as if by chance, let the handcuffs under his jacket jingle.

The woman muttered to herself and then asked:

"Whattaya wanna talk to me about?"

"Signora Lombardo," said Montalbano.

Concetta's attitude suddenly changed. She actually became quite friendly and cordial.

"Come in, come in," she said opening the door wide.

She showed them into the dining room and had them sit down.

"Would you like some coffee?" she asked.

"Sure, why not?" said the inspector.

She left them to themselves, and Montalbano got up and started looking at some framed photographs, all of them of the same good-looking young man: first in a sailor's uniform, then on his wedding day, then high up on a crane.

"That's my son, 'Ntonio. He works in La Spezia," Concetta said proudly, returning with the coffee.

Which was good.

"So whattaya wanna know about the big slut?" Concetta began.

They were off to a good start.

"Why do you call her that?"

"'Cause she's not a honest woman. An' she's shameless, too. She got no—how d'you call it—no modesty! She walks aroun' the house stark nekkid! An' I can tell yiz wha' kind o' condition I foun' the bed in, after certain nights when her husband was away! Juss lookin' at the sheets'd give ya an idea o' wha' was goin' on . . . An' then the husband, the big cornuto, he's never home. Iss almos' like he goes away on purpose so his wife can do all her monkey business!"

"How does Signora Lombardo treat you?"

"Her? I c'n never do nothin' right for the lady! I bust my ass—you'll ascuse th'expression—I bust my ass all mornin' an' she calls me from work to tell me the bathtub's dirty. Natcherly iss gonna be a little dirty wit' all the filth she's doin' inside and outside the tub! An' then she screwed me, the bitch!"

"What do you mean?"

"I mean she just up an' left, 'swas nice knowin' ya, an' din't pay me my lass month!"

"How did you know she went away?"

"'Cause I went to her house an' saw she'd packed a suitcase an' left."

"So you have the house keys?" Montalbano asked.

"Of course. How's I gonna get in otherwise?"

He'd asked a stupid question. This had been happening too often lately.

"Did you ever have a chance to meet the husband?"

Concetta thought about this.

"Maybe ten times over about five months."

"Did he talk to you?"

"Sometimes. But it was always to give orders. He din't kid around, either, when it came to bein' rude."

"What kind of relations were there between the two of them?"

"You mean, did they fuck?"

"Sort of."

"Total strangers."

"In what sense?"

"They didn' even seem like husband and wife."

"Could you explain a little better?"

"Wha' c'n I say? Me, wit' my husband, rest his soul, we used to fight, an' then we'd make up an' then we'd kiss and talk about wha' happened. But those two, nothing . . ."

"Listen, signora, when you were working there, did you ever happen to witness anything strange or unusual—anything, I dunno, that struck you as odd?"

Concetta didn't need to think twice about this.

"One morning we was shot at."

Montalbano started visibly in his chair. Fazio's eyes opened wide.

"Really? Who was shot at?"

"He was, the husband was. The lady wasn't there; she'd already left for work in Montelusa."

"What happened, exactly?"

"Okay, it went like this. He got up late, like aroun' nine thirty or somethin', an' he went into the bat'room. When he came out, since it was a nice day, he tol' me to bring him his coffee ousside, on the veranda. So I went an' made the coffee, an' as I's bringin' it to him, I see him runnin' into the house sayin': 'Don' go ousside, don' go ousside.' So I stopped in the dining room an' he come out o' the bedroom wit' a gun in his hand."

"He had a gun?"

"Yessir, a pistol. Whenever he was home, he'd keep it on his nightstand, which scared me just to look at it, and when he left he'd take it wit' him."

"Go on."

"So he went back to the veranda an' looked ousside. I got a look myself. There was a rubber dinghy with a motor that was moving away. An' there was a hole in the wall on the veranda. Just a quarter inch away from where his head was when he was sittin' down."

"And what did he say to you?"

"That it musta been some kinda mistake."

Adriano and Liliana had been lucky, you had to admit.

"Did anything else happen?"

"Right afterwards, he made a call on his cell phone an' got all pissed off."

"Did you hear what he was saying?"

"I heard everything, but din't understand nothin'."

"Why not?"

"He was talkin' in some foreign language."

"So you understood nothing at all?"

"I caught one name. Nicotra, I think it was."

"When did this happen?"

"Le'ss say about two months ago."

Why were people shooting at a former computer representative?

And why did he keep a pistol within reach?

"Can you tell us anything else, signora?"

"No, there's nothin' else. 'Cept for a kinda fixation they both had."

"And what was that?"

"That I was never supposta go in the little room. The first day I started workin', I went in there to clean. The lady, who was at home that day, started screamin' like a demon an' sayin' I's not supposta ever set foot in that room, for any reason whassoever. But if she din't tell me, how's I supposta know? So she locked the door an' give me a dirty look, and then she put the key in her pocket. The husband used to do the same thing when he was at home."

"So during all that time, you never noticed that the door was open or unlocked?"

"Never."

Montalbano instinctively felt he should press further.

"But didn't you ever feel curious to . . . ?"

"I certainly did."

"And you never wanted to satisfy your curiosity?"

"Well . . ."

"Signora, listen: you would be giving us a great gift if you . . ."

"Oh, all right. One day, I took a hairpin an' . . . It took me a whole hour. An' you know what was in there? Nothin'. A bed, a wardrobe, an' a metal bookcase."

"And what was on the shelves?"

"A few computers an' some printers."

They'd just come out when Fazio's cell phone rang.

"It's Catarella," said Fazio.

Then, a moment later:

"What's going on?"

He stood there for about half a minute, listening, then said:

"All right, all right, we'll be right there."

Then, turning to the inspector:

"I didn't understand a goddamn thing."

Ten minutes later they were standing in front of Catarella, who was all agitated and upset.

"Summon 'at calls 'isself Spinoccia called 'n' said 'e, 'e bein' 'im, meanin' Spinoccia, says 'e foun' a car all boint up by fire inna Melluso districk rounnabout where's the drinkin' truff."

"So you're making all this commotion over a car that burned up?" Montalbano asked.

"No, Chief, all the commission's over the reason whereforats inside it—it bein' it, meanin' the car—'e found—'e bein' still 'im, meanin' Spinoccia—foun' a dead body in cadaveristick condission."

Well, that certainly changed things. Montalbano and Fazio looked at each other.

"Shall we take a squad car?" asked Fazio.

"You take one with Gallo," the inspector replied. "I'll follow behind you in mine."

He went down to the parking lot to wait for Fazio to return with Gallo.

"There's a problem," Fazio said as soon as he reappeared. "Neither me nor Gallo knows where this Melluso district is."

"So what are we going to do?"

"I'll ring City Hall."

At that moment they saw Catarella rushing towards them with his arms raised and yelling.

"Stop! Stop!"

"What is it?" asked Montalbano.

"I tink I made a mistake," said Catarella.

"What kind of mistake?"

"Wha'd I say the districk was?"

"Melluso," the three said in chorus.

"Beckin' yer partin', guys, bu' Melluso's the name odda guy 'at was the one 'oo called. The districk's called Spinoccia."

Montalbano cursed.

"I know where it is," said Gallo, racing towards his car.

"No speeding!" Montalbano shouted at him. "Otherwise I'll never be able to keep up with you."

14

Just outside of town in the direction of Montereale, Gallo turned onto an unpaved road that cut through the open countryside. After going a few miles, he turned left, onto a dirt track that was all humps and holes. It was like being on a boat during a storm.

Despite the warning he'd been given and the terrible condition of the road, Gallo was speeding nonetheless, and Montalbano was having a hard time keeping up.

It was one big cursefest of all the saints in heaven.

After some fifteen minutes of this—during which they didn't see another living soul, not even a bird in flight, aside from a three-legged dog—right before a curve they came upon a man standing in the middle of the road and signaling for them to stop.

They pulled up and got out of their respective cars. Meanwhile, the man approached. He was a peasant of about fifty, tall with a sun-baked face and as thin as a sardine.

"Are you Signor Melluso?" the inspector asked.

"Yessir, I am. Donato Melluso."

"Where's the car?"

"Just past the bend."

The car was in a clearing behind a drinking trough that hadn't seen any water for a good hundred years. The fire had also torched a nearby tree, itself long dry.

All that remained of the car was a metal skeleton turned brown by the flames. It had no license plate, and it was unclear what model it was.

On what must have been the backseat lay a strange black thing, a human body, in a contorted position.

Was it a man or a woman?

Montalbano drew near to have a better look, leaned forward, and only then did the terrible, clinging smell of burnt flesh reach his nostrils.

It wasn't strong. No doubt a good deal of it had already dispersed in the air, which was a sign that the car had been there for a while; still, it was strong enough to make the inspector start gagging.

Before rushing away, he turned to Fazio, who was staring at the scene without moving, and said:

"Alert the whole circus: Pasquano, prosecutor, Forensics . . ."

Then he went up to Melluso.

"When did you discover this?" he asked.

"About an hour and a half ago, at the most. I saw it when I's on my way to my field, an' I went an' had a look, just out of curiosity. I called you as soon as I noticed there was a body inside."

"How did you do that?"

Melluso gave him a confused look.

"How's I supposed to do it? With my cell phone."

And, by way of proof, he dug it out of his pocket.

Montalbano bit his lip. It was one of the many signs of aging, he thought—this refusal to accept that everyone, even anchorite monks, had cell phones these days.

"So the car wasn't here yesterday?"

"I dunno."

"Why not?"

"'Cause I hadn't been out this way for a week, on account of I was sick. I live in Vigàta."

"But doesn't anyone else ever pass along this road?"

"Oh, they pass all right, they pass."

"I'm positive this car's been here for a few days already."

"So?"

"So how do you explain the fact that nobody called us earlier?"

"You're asking me? Y'oughter ask them that surely passed by an' didn't call."

There was something in Melluso's voice that prompted Montalbano to ask him another question.

"How much farther does this road go?"

"'Bout a k'lometer."

"Are there any houses along it?"

"There's two houses. One of 'em belongs to Peppi Lanzetta an' the other to Japico Indelicato."

Without wanting to make it seem so, the man had given Montalbano two pieces of precise information.

The inspector turned away from Melluso and went over to Fazio.

"Did you call?"

"Yessir. But from what I could gather, nobody's going to be here for at least another hour."

"Listen, I'm going to take advantage of the delay and go talk to a couple of people who live here nearby."

"Wait a second, I wanted to tell you something. In my opinion, this man was burned alive."

"How can you tell?"

"He was goat-tied."

"But didn't the fire burn up the rope?"

"They didn't use a rope, but a chain. Come and I'll show you."

"Not on your life," said Montalbano. "I'll take your word for it."

Peppi Lanzetta could have just as easily been sixty years old as ninety. Hoeing the land from dawn to dusk all his life had twisted his body to the point where it looked like a Saracen olive tree.

He wore glasses with lenses half an inch thick.

"No, sir, I din't see nothin'. I ain't left my house for about ten days."

"Don't you ever go into town?"

"What for? I got everything I need. I don't got any family in Vigàta. An' I can't hardly see no more. I'm afraid o' getting' run over by a car."

Japico Indelicato, on the other hand, was a strapping thirty-year-old who didn't seem afraid of anyone.

"No, sir, I don't know anything about any burnt-up car. And I'm telling you the truth. I got nothing to hide. I haven't been into town for three days. But I have to go in tomorrow."

"So three days ago there was no car there?"

"There might've been, but it wasn't burnt up yet."

"What do you mean?"

"Well, I was going down in my old Fiat 500 as it was just getting dark, on my way to dinner at my girlfriend's house, when right around the trough I had to slow down to let two cars pass, which then went and stopped right behind the trough. I'd gone about another fifty yards when my girlfriend called me on my cell phone saying her mother didn't feel too good and so it was better if we did it another time. And so I turned around, and when I passed by the trough the two cars were still there."

"But weren't there any people?"

"Sure there were! There were three people standing outside the cars, talking."

"Did you manage to see their faces?"

"Not really. It was too dark."

"Can you tell me anything about the cars?"

"I'm not too good with car models. All I can say is that one was small and white and the other was big and light brown."

They must have torched the small one.

Disappointed, Montalbano extended his hand to the young man, but Indelicato did not shake it. He hadn't noticed it, lost as he was in thought.

"On the other hand . . ." he said.

"On the other hand?"

"I don't know if it'd be of any use to you."

"Tell me anyway."

"I always play Bancolotto."

And so? What did that have to do with anything?

"Oh yeah?"

"Yessir. And so I memorized the two license plates. Tomorrow I'm gonna go and play those numbers."

The inspector rejoiced.

"You have the license plates?!"

"Not all of them, just the numbers."

Better than nothing.

"Let me have them."

The young man pulled a small piece of paper out of his pocket.

"I wrote them down afterwards. The number of the small car was 225; and the big car, 866."

Montalbano wrote them down on a piece of paper.

"I'm gonna play a straight tern," said the young man. "Twenty-two, fifty-eight, and sixty-six."

"Best of luck," said Montalbano.

But Japico Indelicato didn't reply. He was lost in thought again.

"I'm just remembering . . ." he said.

Montalbano didn't breathe a word.

"When I stopped to let the cars by, I read the license plate on the first car, which was the small one, but then I was also able to read the number on the big car, too, by looking in the rearview mirror."

Another game of mirrors.

"And aside from the numbers, the letters on the big car's plate made me think of something . . . but right now I can't remember what it was."

"If it comes back to you, could you call me?"

"Absolutely."

When he drove past the trough again, the inspector saw that the circus hadn't arrived yet, and so he waved bye-bye to Fazio and kept on going.

What was he doing there anyway?

On his way to the station, he felt restless and troubled. Something was spinning around in his head, but he couldn't grasp what it was.

"Any news, Cat?"

"Nuttin', Chief."

"Is Inspector Augello here?"

"Yessir, 'e's onna premisses."

"Send 'im to me."

Mimì walked in triumphantly.

"Do you want me to sing the march from *Aida*?" said Montalbano.

Augello didn't even hear him.

"O ye of little faith!"

"Tell me everything."

"I sent out the search notice, and barely five minutes later they called me from San Cataldo."

"And wha'd they say?"

"That Adriano Lombardo was stopped by a Road Police patrol for speeding. He was on his way back from Catania."

"Did they let him go?"

"Of course. What did you expect, that they would arrest him? He'll get slapped with a nice fine and lose a few points on his license. But, if nothing else, we now know he hasn't left the island and he's still in the neighborhood."

"But did they get his address?"

"Come on. Albergo Trinacria, Caltanissetta."

"Did you try calling?"

"Of course. They told me Signor Lombardo checked out this morning."

"Did you ask if he was alone?"

"What kind of question is that? He was alone."

Which meant simply that the inspector had been wrong.

Liliana had not hooked up with her husband, who seemed to have turned into the Scarlet Pimpernel.

"I'm sure we'll be getting other reports soon," Mimì reassured him.

It was time to go home to Marinella. But first he wanted to ring Fazio.

"How are we doing?"

"They're all still here, Chief, and we're waiting for the generator with the floodlights. It's getting dark and we can't see a thing. We'll probably be here till morning."

"Sorry about that."

The moment he got home, he felt an overwhelming need to take a shower. He also thought he'd been wearing the same suit for too many days and it was time to have it cleaned and pressed.

And so he removed all the sheets and scraps of paper he found in his jacket pockets—there were even some rolled up in the inside breast pocket—and set them all down on the dining room table. Then he went into the bathroom, took a long shower, put on just a pair of underpants, opened the armoire, pulled out a clean suit, and put it on the chair beside the bed.

And since it was hot—not quite as hot as the previous days but still hot—he decided not to put any more clothes on. After all, he wasn't expecting any visitors, and it was unlikely anyone would be passing by on the beach when he sat down on the veranda to eat.

But before setting the table, he decided to look at the papers he'd taken out of his pockets. It was a sort of weekly chore he did, and it was almost certain that, as had happened so many times before, at least half of those papers and scraps would end up in the wastebasket, and many others would have no more meaning for him.

He pulled up a chair and sat down. On the first piece of paper that his gaze fell upon, there were a couple of words and a number. *Droop to 165*. He felt bewildered. What on earth was that supposed to mean? The handwriting was his, no doubt about it.

Why had he felt the need to write down such an incomprehensible phrase? And what did the number 165 mean?

At that moment the phone rang. It was Livia.

"I'm calling you now because later I'm going to the movies with a friend."

"Have fun," he said gruffly.

"What's with you?"

Droop to 165, that's what.

"Nothing. I'm irritated because I was going through my papers and I found a note that I'm unable to decipher."

"Can I be of help?"

"How?"

"Well, you could read it to me, for starters."

"Droop to one sixty-five."

Livia laughed. Montalbano got upset.

"I'd like to know what's so funny!"

"It's not 'droop,' silly!"

"How do you know?"

"Because we talked about it the other night."

Montalbano was incredulous.

"You and I talked the other night about drooping—"

"No! The word isn't 'droop.' I think you meant to write 'drop.'"

She was right. Now he remembered everything. Livia had told him that his body mass index was such and such, that he should therefore eat less and bring his weight down to 165, and he must have distractedly made a note of it.

They chatted for another five minutes, then said good night. Montalbano went back to looking at his papers.

He picked up a small scrap.

Suzuki GK 225 RT.

He very nearly fell out of his chair. This was the license plate number of Liliana's car, which the mechanic had given to him.

He started frantically searching through all the scraps of paper until he found the note with the license plate numbers Japico Indelicato had given him. According to

Indelicato, the number of the smaller car, the one that had been torched, was 225. The exact same number the mechanic had given him.

This was the thought that had been tormenting him on his way back from Spinoccia and he hadn't been able to bring it into focus.

It was 99 percent certain that the burnt car was Liliana's.

He grabbed the telephone and called Fazio.

"Send me Gallo with the car, would you?"

He didn't feel like driving at night over that treacherous dirt road.

He leapt to his feet, got dressed in a hurry—shirt, jeans, and jacket.

Gallo arrived half an hour later.

You could see the glow of the floodlights from afar. They made a luminous aura in the sky.

They were all still there on the premises, as Catarella would have said. Apparently the people with the generator had only just shown up.

Fazio came running up to the inspector.

"What's going on?" he asked.

"It's possible the torched car is Liliana's."

The inspector showed him the two scraps of paper and explained everything.

"Have they pulled the body out yet?"

"No. Forensics hasn't finished taking samples. The prosecutor gave permission to remove it and then left."

"Is Dr. Pasquano here?"

"He's locked up inside his car. He's furious because he lost at poker again."

"Listen, I don't want to have anything to do with Arquà. See if you can find out whether the car is a Suzuki."

He waited for Fazio to finish talking with the chief of Forensics, then steeled his nerves and headed over to Dr. Pasquano's car.

Despite the heat, the doctor had all the windows up and was immersed in a dense cloud of smoke.

Montalbano tapped on the car door. Pasquano looked up, recognized him, and then articulated quite clearly:

"Do-not-bust-my-balls!"

"Just one minute!"

The doctor opened the door and got out of the car.

"I was told you'd gone home, and so I breathed a sigh of relief. But no! Here he is again, the good inspector, back to singe my short and curlies!"

"Have you had a look at the body?"

"You call that thing a body? It's just a piece of charcoal! I'd like to see you identify it!"

"I might be of some help."

"How? By telling me the story of Snow White and the Seven Dwarves?"

"No, by telling you I think I know who it is."

"Oh, really? Then please do enlighten me with the

fruit of your elucubrations, though I have my doubts, given the deteriorating state of your brain due to your advanced age."

Montalbano let the provocation slide.

"It's probably a youth not much more than twenty years old, and I know his name, address, and family."

"What the hell do I care about his family?"

"I was just telling you, to save time. In case we need to resort to DNA testing to identify him."

"Jesus, how well spoken you are tonight! I'm glad."

At that moment some sort of nurse came over to Pasquano.

"Doctor, we can take the body out now, if that's all right with you," the person said.

Pasquano walked away with the nurse without saying anything to Montalbano, who headed over to the squad car. Fazio pulled up beside him.

"Arquà says it's not beyond the realm of possibility that it's a Suzuki. But he needs to check some other things."

"I'm convinced of it. Just as I'm convinced that the charred body in there is Arturo Tallarita."

"I'm of the same opinion."

"Things didn't go the way you and I had thought," said the inspector. "Liliana may have wanted to reach her husband, but she didn't make it; they intercepted her first."

"Apparently they were keeping an eye on her," said Fazio.

"Yeah. And if they burned the kid alive, that means they'd kept him prisoner for a few days. Maybe even together with Liliana, who we now know—assuming she's still alive—is in the hands of the people who shot at her."

"But what do you think this all means?"

"If we forget Arturo Tallarita for just a moment—since I think he's a case entirely apart, though I may be wrong—what we're seeing is the extreme pressure these people are putting on Adriano Lombardo through his wife."

"And what might they hope to gain?"

"For him either to do or not do something."

"And what could that be?"

Montalbano threw his hands up.

"I'm totally in the dark. But I do think I'm beginning to understand a few things."

"Shall I have someone take you home?" Fazio asked.

"No, I'll go and wait in the car till you're done."

They didn't finish until two in the morning.

15

Between one thing and another he managed to get to bed by quarter past three, and as soon as he closed his eyes, he passed out as if he'd been clubbed in the head, sinking into a fathomless sleep, an utter nothingness of total darkness and sidereal silence.

Then, after a little while, inside that nothingness, a constant, annoying sound, sort of like a drill, began to bore its way into his mind, starting at first very far away, then becoming gradually louder and louder.

At a certain point it grew so shrill and close that it became unbearable and woke him up.

But when he opened his eyes, the sound, instead of vanishing, as happens with dreams, was still there, as insistent as ever.

He turned on the light and looked at his watch. Four o'clock. He'd slept a scant forty-five minutes.

He felt completely addled, lacking the coordinates for

orienting himself in time and space, still half blanketed under the cloak of sleep, and it wasn't until the irritating sound stopped that he was able to realize that what had woken him up was a siren.

He waited for someone to ring the doorbell, convinced that it was Gallo coming to pick him up because something big had happened.

But no one rang.

He got up and went to open the French door that gave onto the veranda.

To the left, the beach looked like it was moving, undulating, and this was because it was lit up by a great heaving blaze that could only be coming from the Lombardos' house.

This was all he could see from where he was standing, but it was enough to tell him that their house was going up in flames.

He dashed into the bedroom, put his jeans and shirt back on, and opened his front door.

Now he could see the flashing red lights of the fire trucks and cars and heard frantic voices shouting commands.

He rushed over.

Though he was sure he was awake, he felt as if he were still dreaming. The flashing lights, the shadows of the firemen, the silhouettes of the cars made the whole thing seem sort of artificial, rather like a film set.

He felt as if he were running in slow motion.

"I'm Inspector Montalbano. I live in the house next door," he said to a fire sergeant. "What's going on?"

The guy must have recognized him.

"Ah, yes," he said. "Good morning, Inspector. We were alerted by someone driving by on the main road who thought he saw the beginnings of a fire in this house. It took us only twenty minutes to get here from Monte-lusa. The part that's in flames is on the side by the sea."

Montalbano knew that about fifty yards ahead there was a passage that gave access to the beach. He covered the distance at a run, then turned around and started walking back across the sand towards the Lombardo house.

When he got there, he saw that the fire, which had consumed the veranda and also set upon the French door, was already dying down, thanks to the powerful jets of water from the fire hoses.

The sergeant he'd spoken to earlier came up to him.

"We were lucky to get here in time. If not for the phone call, the whole house would have burned down."

A question occurred to Montalbano.

"Did the person give his name?"

"No, they wanted to remain anonymous."

Anybody's guess why.

"Do you know if there was anyone in the house?" the fireman asked.

"I don't think so."

"Still, it's always better to check."

"Antò, could you come over here a minute?" one of

the firemen rummaging through the debris of the veranda called out to the sergeant.

The two chattered a bit in low voices.

The fireman was folding some strange, unidentifiable object. Then the sergeant turned to the inspector.

"It looks like arson," he said. "My colleague found the remains of a jerry can of gasoline."

Montalbano had already thought of that scenario. But what could it mean?

"I'm going to have them remove the French door, which is still burning, and then go inside," said the fire sergeant.

"May I come with you?"

The question had come out before he knew it.

"If you wish . . ."

They got going. The lights didn't work; there'd probably been a short circuit. The fire sergeant asked for a large flashlight and they went in.

The dining room was full of dense, viscous smoke that had turned all the surfaces black.

Same in the hallway. The door to the extra room was locked. The fire sergeant opened it with a sort of passepartout he kept in his belt. In this room there was hardly any smoke, and the bed, wardrobe, and shelves with computers remained relatively clean.

They headed for the bedroom, the sergeant leading the way with the flashlight and the inspector following behind.

When he reached the doorway, the fire sergeant did two things in rapid succession: he first gave a stifled cry and then leapt backwards, the flashlight falling from his hands and going out.

Montalbano, also reeling backwards as the sergeant's body collided with his, didn't understand what was happening.

"What is it?" he asked.

"There's somebody on the bed," the sergeant said, bending down to look for the flashlight.

Montalbano froze. Who could it be?

Could it be Lombardo, holed up in his house the whole time everyone was searching for him over land and sea?

Was he asleep?

And why hadn't he woken up with all the mayhem around him?

At last the fire sergeant found his flashlight and lit up the room.

Liliana's naked body lay facedown across soot-blackened sheets partly stained red with the blood that had clearly come from her slit throat.

The wound wasn't visible, but it was clear they had slashed her throat.

Her clothes lay on a chair near the bed.

Montalbano stood stock-still, a high-tension current running up his spine.

He couldn't make any connections; only dribs and drabs of ideas raced through his head. One train of thought would break off all of a sudden, followed by another even more short-lived.

"I'd better call this in," the fire sergeant said with a quavering voice.

"I'll join you in a minute," said the inspector. "Leave me the flashlight."

He wanted to check whether his impression had been correct. He went up to the bed and touched the sheet. The blood on it was still wet.

Liliana had been murdered that same night.

But why had they brought her home to kill her? And if one thing was certain, it was that they'd set fire to the house so the body would be discovered immediately.

And the anonymous caller who'd phoned the fire department was the same person who'd set the house on fire. He'd wanted to make sure the body wasn't destroyed by the flames.

Montalbano went back to his house, quickly washed himself, got dressed again, in his best clothes, grabbed his cigarettes, and started smoking outside his front door while waiting for his men to come and pick him up.

Liliana's murder hadn't surprised him. Actually, he'd thought they'd done away with her some time ago.

But seeing her butchered on the bed like that had un-leashed a great swell of melancholy in him that he was unable to shake off.

His men's car, with Gallo at the wheel accompanied by Fazio, didn't stop at the Lombardos' house but went on until it pulled up right in front of him. At his feet were a good ten crushed cigarette butts.

Fazio rushed out of the car.

"I didn't really understand," he said. "Who was it that was killed?"

"Liliana," said the inspector. "They slit her throat."

Fazio gave a start. Then he lowered his voice.

"But she wasn't there yesterday!"

"Well, she's there now."

"But why?"

Montalbano changed the subject.

"Have you alerted everyone?"

"Yessir. You wouldn't believe the cursing. They'd all just got back home and undressed before they had to get dressed again and go back out."

"Listen. I'm gonna stay here," said Montalbano. "If you need me, just call."

"You don't want to be present?"

"Are you kidding? With a beautiful dead woman be-fore his eyes, and naked to boot, Prosecutor Tommaseo's gonna go nuts! He'll ask me ten thousand questions! Don't forget, he also saw the footage of the failed scoop."

"Yeah, you're right."

"Oh, and one thing. When he's done, I want to talk to Pasquano. Try to talk him into coming over here to see me. Tell him I'll make him a cup of good coffee."

After some two hours sitting out on the veranda and drinking two mugfuls of coffee, he heard a knock at the door. It was Pasquano.

The doctor came in muttering to himself.

"I'm warning you that even if they kill half of Vigàta over the course of the day, I'm not setting foot out of my house!" Then, looking at the inspector askance, he threatened: "And I truly hope, for your own good, that the coffee you promised me is excellent."

"I made it just now."

Montalbano sat him down on the veranda.

"My compliments," said Pasquano. "You have a lovely house." Then he added: "And you used to have a lovely neighbor."

Montalbano went on the offensive:

"What can you tell me about her?"

The doctor gave him an indignant look.

"And you think you can buy me with a barely drinkable cup of coffee?"

"You must be kidding! A man of your unshakable

integrity? Though I might try to buy you with a second cup and a cigarette."

"It's a deal."

The doctor sipped his second coffee and fired up a cigarette.

"It's going to be rough on you," he said.

"On me?" asked the inspector.

"Yeah. But I wasn't referring to the murder. I was thinking—with great compassion, mind you—of how hard it's going to be for you in just a few years when you have to leave this beautiful house and move to an old folks' home."

The doctor was being his usual obnoxious self. The inspector had to return fire, or the assault might never end.

"I don't think it'll be so bad at the old folks' home, since we'll probably be sharing a room," Montalbano replied. "We can play poker with some of the nurses. You'll probably have a better chance of winning with them."

Pasquano laughed heartily, indicating he was probably satisfied with the riposte.

"So what can you tell me?"

"I'll grant you three questions."

"When was she killed?"

"This very night, between twelve and two, two thirty."

"You're sure about that?"

"The only sure things in life, as you know, are death and taxes. But with my experience, it's unlikely I'm wrong."

"Was her throat slit?"

"Yes, a single cut. But . . ."

"But?"

"Probably not done all at once, but slowly. With a very sharp blade, probably a straight razor."

"Were there any bruises or hematomas or other marks around the wrists and ankles?"

Pasquano looked at him suspiciously.

"You seem to know the whole story already. Did you know her?"

"Yes."

"In the biblical sense?"

"No."

"They must have kept her tied up a long time," said Pasquano.

"Thanks," said the inspector.

"Is that all?" asked Pasquano, disappointed. "Aren't you going to ask me the same thing Tommaseo asked me immediately?"

"All right, I'll ask you. Was she raped?"

"To all appearances, yes. But I'll have a better sense of it after I examine her."

"Can I ask one last question?"

"I'm feeling generous this morning."

"Did they rape her when she was still alive or after she was dead?"

"In my opinion, as she was dying."

Montalbano felt his stomach twist into a knot.

Fazio sort of relieved Dr. Pasquano. His exhaustion was written all over his face.

"They've all left, thank God. The house has been cordoned off and sealed."

"Want some coffee?"

"Hell yes!"

He sipped it slowly, savoring every drop.

"Thanks. If not for that, I'd be already asleep."

"What do you make of it all?"

"Well, I was almost certain they would kill her, after they'd shown they were capable of burning Tallarita alive."

"Then you should know that, according to Pasquano, they raped her as they were slitting her throat."

Fazio shuddered as though cold.

"Animals."

"But who could they be, in your opinion?"

Fazio threw up his hands.

"For my part, I've been getting an idea, these last few hours," said Montalbano.

"Really?"

"Yeah, but I'm not gonna tell you just yet."

"I just can't figure out why they brought her here to kill her," said Fazio.

"I can. And it was a big mistake."

Fazio gave him a bewildered look.

"How?"

"They've allowed me to see the whole thing in a new light, which is a big help."

"Well, don't just let me sit here dying of curiosity," said Fazio.

"As soon as you get to headquarters," said Montalbano, "I want you to issue an urgent, top-priority search bulletin for Lombardo. The sooner we find him the better—for him, that is. If we waste any more time, we may still find him, but he'll be dead, too."

Fazio gave him a look of dismay.

━━━

"Chief, 'at'd be Signor Doctor Pisquano onna line."

Who of course was Pasquano.

"What? Hadn't you told me you'd be staying at home all day?" Montalbano asked, immediately going on the attack.

"Well, that's just how bloody senile I've become! Instead of going home to rest I went straight as a rocket to the institute!"

"So it's possible you have more to tell me about the murder victim."

"No, she has to wait her turn! I've been working on the lad."

"And what can you tell me?"

"I don't think there's any need for DNA testing."

"Oh no? Why not?"

"I'm told you know his family in some way?"

"That's correct."

"Could you find out whether he had by any chance fractured his left arm as a child?"

"I'll do it straightaway. But tell me something."

"You have to say 'please' first. Weren't you ever taught any manners? Or have you forgotten them all in your old age?"

Patience, Montalbà.

"I would like you *please* to tell me whether the kid was alive when they set fire to the car."

"Yes, he was. But he must have died before the flames got to him, from strangulation, since he'd been goat-tied."

Montalbano didn't feel up to seeing the anguished, grief-stricken face of poor Signora Tallarita again.

He sent Officer Mancuso, who was a man of a certain age with a gentle manner.

"Try to find out whether the son, Arturo, broke his arm when he was a little kid. But don't ask her directly, or she'll get alarmed. Ask her a whole slew of questions, tell her that the more details we have, the more likely it is that we'll find him."

He had a positive answer in barely half an hour. Arturo had broken his arm when he was ten.

He called Dr. Pasquano to tell him.

Then he went out to eat, even though it was still early and he wasn't hungry. If nothing else, it would help pass the time.

Enzo was intently watching the midday TeleVigàta news report. Ragonese was just finishing his editorial.

There is a rumor going around in well-informed circles that this ghastly crime will have clamorous and unthinkable consequences. Apparently it involves individuals who until now had been considered above suspicion. But as strict observers of professional protocol, we shall say no more on this pressing subject until our information is verifiably certain. Naturally, we will promptly notify our viewers of any new developments as they emerge.

Montalbano started laughing. These people were making one mistake after another. Ragonese's words were an indirect confirmation of the truth he had started to glimpse.

He suddenly felt hungry.

"What can I get for you, Inspector?"

"Give me everything you've got."

"I see you came full of good intentions."

As a result, he took his walk along the jetty at a slow pace and then sat on the flat rock for a long time, thinking about what his next move should be. He couldn't afford to make a mistake. This time there was no crab, but still he thought he'd come up with the right idea. And so he returned to the office.

Upon entering, he said to Catarella:

"Get someone else to man the switchboard and then come into my office."

"Straightaways, Chief."

Five minutes later there was a knock.

"Yer orders, Chief."

"Come in, close the door, and have a seat."

Catarella closed the door, but instead of sitting down, he remained standing at attention in front of the desk.

"Cat, I can't talk to you with you standing that way. You look like a puppet in the puppet theatre. Sit down."

"Bein' in yer presence like diss, poissonally in poisson, it woudna seem right to me, Chief; I woudna wanna make no offense like."

"Sit down; that's an order."

Catarella obeyed.

"What are you doing this evening?"

"Me?!"

"Yes, you."

"Chief, whattaya aspeck me to do? I'm gonna watch TV an' try an' finnish a crossword puzzle I been woikin' on f'r a month."

"I see. And what time do you usually go to bed?"

"Rounnabout minnight, Chief."

Catarella was sweating, but he didn't dare ask the inspector to explain the reason for this poissonal interrogation.

16

"Are you prepared to lose a few hours of sleep tonight?" the inspector continued.

Catarella sprang to his feet.

His face was flushed and a slight tremor was running through his entire body.

"Chief, I'd be assolutely perpared a go a whole mont' wittout shuttin' my eyes f'yiz, Chief! D'I say a mont'? A whole year! E'en more, Chief, till ya come an' say t'me, 'Cat, iss time to go to bed!'"

Montalbano almost started to get emotional.

"All right, then, at midnight tonight I want you to be at my place in Marinella."

"Yes, sir!"

"And bring whatever tools you'd need to fix a computer."

"Ayeayeaye sah!"

"And don't tell anyone."

"I's silent azza grave, Chief!"

"You can go back to the switchboard now."

Catarella moved towards the door, but without managing to bend at the knees. He really did look like a puppet. Such was the effect of his happiness at being assigned a secret mission by Montalbano.

An hour later, Catarella rang him.

"Chief, 'at'd be yer frenn onna line, Pito, the joinalist frenna yiz."

It was Nicolò Zito.

"I urgently need to talk to you."

"What is it?"

"Not over the telephone. If I come by in half an hour at the latest, will you still be at the office?"

"Yes. But I can probably spare you the trip. I think I know what you want to talk to me about."

"Did you see Ragonese's report?"

"Yes."

"Did you understand who he was referring to?"

"Perfectly."

"Are you sure you understood?"

"He was referring to me."

"So what are you going to do? Do you want me to interview you? My TV station is at your disposal."

"You're a true friend, I know that. But how did you find out?"

"An anonymous phone call."

"They must have done the same with Ragonese."

"Right. So what do you want to do?"

"Nothing, for the moment."

"As you wish."

No, this time Montalbano really wanted to see how far other people's faith in him went.

As he was about to leave for Marinella, another phone call came in from Pasquano.

When had such a phenomenon ever occurred before? Was there going to be an earthquake? Armageddon?

"Tell me sincerely, Doctor, do you suddenly have the hots for me?"

The reply came fast.

"Do you really think that if I decided to take such a leap to the other shore, I would settle for an old geezer like you?"

The civilities could now be considered over.

"To what do I owe the honor?"

"Didn't I already tell you that today is my day for being generous? I've just finished working on the woman."

"Any news?"

"None. Just confirmation of everything I said before. She was kept bound for a long time, was murdered between midnight and two a.m., and was raped in a particularly brutal fashion. They actually wounded and penetrated her with a knife. But there was no ejaculation. Odd, wouldn't you say?"

If what Montalbano was thinking was right, it wasn't odd at all.

On the contrary.

It was another confirmation.

He went home. Adelina had prepared a big platter of eggplant parmesan. He savored it on the veranda, eating it slowly to allow the flavor on the palate enough time to reach his heart, brain, and soul.

Then he went inside, turned on the television, and tuned in to TeleVigàta. Pippo Ragonese talked about the problems caused by the closure of two factories in the province and declared himself certain that the government would intervene in a timely fashion and that the laid-off workers would be relocated in new jobs.

Yeah, right, thought Montalbano.

Of the Lombardo murder, only the briefest of mentions was made at the end of the report:

The rumors concerning clamorous new developments in the case are rapidly intensifying. We are confident we shall soon be in a position to give our viewers a full report. For now, however, to put you on the right path, we invite you to view the upcoming program in our broadcast day, a superb film starring the unforgettable Gian Maria Volonté, Investigation of a Citizen Above Suspicion. *Have a good evening, and enjoy the film.*

Montalbano remembered the film well. Volonté plays a police inspector who murders his mistress and then purposely leads the investigation astray. Ragonese was a clever sonofabitch.

He changed the channel and started watching a film with one gunfight after another. At eleven o'clock he turned the TV off, got up, went into the kitchen, grabbed a pair of latex gloves, put them on, put his bunch of skeleton keys in his pocket along with a flashlight, and went out of the house, leaving the door slightly ajar. He didn't want Catarella to know where the things he was going to work on came from. To avoid being seen by any motorists driving by on the main road, he went to the Lombardo house by way of the beach and would return by the same route. He was unable to enter through the veranda door, however. It had been boarded up with planks. He had no choice but to enter through the front door, at the risk of being seen.

"If somebody sees me, Ragonese certainly won't let slip an opportunity to say that the killer always returns to the scene of the crime," he thought as he was removing the seals.

He didn't shine the flashlight into the bedroom. Even though he knew Liliana's body was no longer on the bed, he was sure that he would still see her there, naked, and with her throat slit. It wasn't the sort of image you could get quickly out of your head.

Some forty minutes later, he set a computer and a printer down on his dining room table. Beside them he laid the latex gloves.

Catarella arrived punctually carrying a briefcase. He was so worked up that he couldn't get his words out.

"A . . . awa . . . awa . . . yer . . . orders, Chief!"

Montalbano took him into the dining room.

"Sit down, Cat."

"Izzat an order?"

"It's an order."

Catarella obeyed.

"Put these gloves on."

Catarella put them on.

"Now take this computer apart."

"Straightaways, Chief. But if ya stay 'ere watchin' me whilst I woik i' makes me noivous."

"I'll go out on the veranda and smoke."

He went outside. He wasn't the least bit worried. In fact, he was convinced he was on the right track.

After five minutes had passed, he heard Catarella cry out in wonder.

"*Matre santa*, Chief! Come 'n' see!"

Montalbano didn't move. He didn't need to go and see. He already knew what Catarella had found.

"Now put the computer back together, and the printer, too," he said from the veranda.

Forty-five minutes later, after Catarella had left, he

took the computer back to the Lombardo house, put the seals back in place, then went home to bed and slept the sleep of the just.

The frantic ringing of the doorbell woke him up. The first light of dawn shone through the window. He looked at his watch. Quarter to seven. The person ringing seemed to have forgotten his finger on the button.

The inspector yawned, stretched, got out of bed, and slipped on a pair of underpants.

"Coming!"

When he opened the door he found a uniformed police officer of his acquaintance, whom he knew to be in the employ of the commissioner's office of Montelusa. Behind him was a squad car with another cop at the wheel.

"Good morning, sir. I've come on orders of the commissioner to pick you up. He wants to see you immediately."

Montalbano didn't want to appear the least bit surprised at being summoned at that hour of the morning.

"Let me take a shower and get dressed. I'll be quick. In the meantime, if you'd like to come in and sit down . . ."

"No, thank you."

He left the door ajar and put a pot of coffee on the stove, shaved, drank the coffee, got into the shower, and got dressed.

He couldn't refrain, every so often, from laughing to himself. The clamorous consequences predicted by that asshole Ragonese were beginning.

"Here I am, all ready to go."

He locked his front door, the uniformed cop gestured to him to get in the backseat, and they drove off. The driver turned on the siren and started speeding worse than Gallo. But did they all have the same vice? Why did they drive so fast when there was no need?

Sitting in one of the two chairs in front of C'mishner Bonetti-Alderighi's desk was Vanni Arquà, chief of Forensics. This was something Montalbano had expected.

"Please sit down," said the commissioner.

He was wearing a dark expression.

Montalbano settled into the other chair. He and Arquà didn't even exchange greetings.

"I'll get right to the point," said the commissioner.

But he didn't. First he opened and closed a drawer of his desk, then he stared at the tip of a pencil as though not knowing what it was for, and finally he said:

"It's better if you talk, Arquà."

The chief of Forensics stared at his shoe tops as he spoke.

"When taking evidence samples from the Lombardo house, we found a great many of your fingerprints."

"How did you know they were mine?" asked Montalbano.

"The way I always do. I compared them. All of our fingerprints are on file."

"I see. So, as soon as you saw the fingerprints taken from the house, you said to yourself: Want to bet these are Montalbano's? And indeed they were. Congratulations on your intuition. So tell me: Is that the way it went?"

He knew that it couldn't be the way it went. But he wanted to know who had put the idea in Arquà's head. And, in fact, Arquà squirmed uncomfortably in his chair and looked at the commissioner.

Who decided to intervene.

"Late yesterday morning, Dr. Arquà received an anonymous letter. He turned it over to me immediately, and I read it and gave him authorization to compare the fingerprints. He acted quite correctly. If you want to read the letter . . ."

He pulled it out of a drawer and held it out for Montalbano. Who didn't reach out to take it, and did not even move.

"Don't you want to read it?"

"I'm sorry, but I find it rather distasteful to read anonymous letters, especially first thing in the morning. At any rate, I don't need to read it. I can easily imagine the contents. It says that I was madly in love with Signora Lombardo, kept her prisoner in her house while conducting searches for her far and wide, and finally, the other night, slit her throat after raping her. And then I set fire to her house in the hopes of destroying all trace of my repeated visits. Have I guessed right?"

"Yes," said the commissioner.

He'd imagined that was the way it was, but to hear it confirmed made him start to seethe with rage.

He turned to Arquà but his words were for other ears.

"And you, Arquà, you felt no shame at lending credence to an anonymous letter? Are you aware that a copy of this defamatory letter was sent to Pippo Ragonese the TV journalist, who now expects 'clamorous consequences'?"

"It certainly wasn't me who sent it," said Arquà.

"I don't doubt that for an instant. It was the murderers themselves who sent it, and in whom you place such trust."

Arquà didn't react. The commissioner was studying the ceiling intently. The inspector turned to him.

"Excuse me, sir, but did you inform Dr. Arquà that I'd already been inside the house, having been invited there by Signora Lombardo, and that I was the victim of attempted blackmail on that occasion?"

"Yes, and I also told him that there was an investigation in progress being conducted by Prosecutor Tommaseo."

"So of course you found my fingerprints there!"

This time it was Bonetti-Alderighi who looked at the chief of Forensics.

"There's one fingerprint in particular that cannot be from the evening you went there to dinner," said Arquà.

"Oh yeah? And where'd you get it?"

"From the bloodstained sheet on the bed."

It was true! He'd touched the sheet after asking the fire sergeant for the flashlight, to check whether the blood was dry or not. But he was alone at that moment; there were no witnesses. It was a stupid fucking mistake.

No matter what he said, there was no guarantee they would believe him. He decided to change tactics.

"Well?" said the commissioner. "How do you explain it?"

A little theatre at this point might not hurt. But was it really theatre? Or did he feel genuinely offended at being suspected of murder? He shot to his feet, twisted his face up into a frown, and spoke in an angry tone.

"In short, it seems you both believe me capable of such a revolting murder. All I can do at this point is make two requests. The first is to have Dr. Arquà take one of those psychiatric tests similar to the one that you, Mr. Commissioner, had me subjected to!"

Bonetti-Alderighi looked flummoxed.

"I had you take a psychiatric test?! When?"

"I don't know, maybe I dreamed it, but it's the same thing."

"How is it the same thing?!"

"It is! Haven't you ever read *Life Is a Dream* by Calderón de la Barca? My second request is: I want my lawyer! I won't answer any more of your questions until my lawyer is present!"

He sat back down, pulled out a handkerchief, and wiped his brow, though there wasn't a drop of sweat on it.

Bonetti-Alderighi and Arquà exchanged glances.

"Good God, Montalbano, nobody's accusing you of anything!" said the commissioner. "We're just trying to clear up—"

"On the basis of an anonymous letter?"

"No!" said Arquà. "On the basis of a fingerprint for which you haven't been able to give us an explanation."

So that was the conclusion? Did Bonetti-Alderighi and Arquà really believe what they were saying? Montalbano was beginning to feel overwhelmed by a blind rage. Should he react now or wait and embarrass their asses later? He chose the second option and remained silent.

"For the time being, let's do this," said the commissioner. "You, Montalbano, are relieved of all ongoing investigations, effective immediately. And you're excused from duty. But you must remain available. I shall turn your investigations of the two crimes over to the chief of the Flying Squad."

Without a word, and without taking leave, Montalbano stood up and left the room.

But as soon as he was outside, he turned and went back into the room, striding decisively up to the commis-

sioner's desk. The two men were looking at him open-
mouthed.

"I forgot to tell you one little detail: I have an ironclad
alibi," he said.

"And what's that?" asked the commissioner.

"Have you read the report that Dr. Pasquano sent
you?"

"I've got it here on my desk, but I haven't had time
yet," the commissioner replied, taking it out from a pile of
other papers and starting to read it.

"And how about you?" he turned and asked Arquà.

"Me neither."

"So you both chose to read an anonymous letter rather
than the coroner's report. If you'd be so kind, Mr. Commissioner, to read out loud at what time the doctor says
the murder was committed . . ."

"Here it says between midnight and two a.m.," said
the commissioner.

"Very well. At that hour I was in the district of Spinoccia, where the dead body of—"

"You're lying!" Arquà exclaimed angrily. "I was there
and I didn't see you!"

"Be careful what you say, Arquà. You've already made
the commissioner look bad; don't make things worse. Did
Fazio come over to you to ask whether the burnt-up car
might be a Suzuki?"

"Yes, but that doesn't mean you were present!"

"Mr. Commissioner, I will give you the names of the people who can testify that I was in Spinoccia that night, but only on the condition that Dr. Arquà is not present. Otherwise I shall institute legal proceedings to defend myself from this ignoble accusation."

The commissioner didn't hesitate for a second. He realized that things were taking a nasty turn.

"Would you please step outside?" he asked Arquà.

Palefaced, the chief of Forensics stood up and went out.

"Officer Gallo, Inspector Fazio, Dr. Pasquano, and an orderly from the Forensic Medicine Institute can confirm that between midnight and two a.m. I was in the district of Spinoccia and therefore could not have raped and murdered Signora Lombardo," Montalbano said all in one breath.

"But why did they try to implicate you?" asked the commissioner.

"So the case would be taken out of my hands. As was in fact about to happen. Maybe they're beginning to suspect that I'm just a step away from the truth. But I don't think the whole setup was premeditated. The people who torched young Tallarita alive are the same who held Signora Lombardo prisoner. The night of the murder they must have driven by on the main road, from which you can see my house. In the trunk they had poor Liliana Lombardo and were surely taking her to her place of execution. But when they saw my car parked in front of my house, they drew the logical conclusion that I was at home sleeping. And so they decided to kill Signora Lombardo in her own home and to rape her, though without ejaculating, so that I could be suspected of that, too, since we wouldn't be able to do a DNA test that would have cleared me of everything. Except that I was not, in fact, at home. I'd had Officer Gallo come and pick me up and take me to Spinoccia."

"I didn't quite understand what you said to Arquà about an anonymous letter supposedly sent to Ragonese."

"I don't actually know whether it was a letter or an anonymous phone call, but Ragonese started talking about clamorous developments and even mentioned a film in which a police inspector murders his mistress . . . Clearly he wants revenge for the failed scoop."

"What can I do?"

"A generic disavowal would suffice."

"I'll do it at once," said the commissioner. "But . . ."

He had a question on the tip of his tongue but not the courage to ask it. Montalbano understood.

"As for the fingerprint on the bedsheet, Dr. Arquà had no way of knowing that once the blaze had been brought under control, I went inside the house together with a sergeant of the Fire Department. I wanted to check whether the blood on the sheet was still fresh. The fire sergeant could certainly confirm my story."

Bonetti-Alderighi stood up and held out his hand.

"Thanks for your understanding," he said.

"No problem," said Montalbano.

And to work off all the agitation that had built up inside him, he decided to get off the bus back to Vigàta at the station for the temples, and walked very slowly the rest of the way.

17

By the time he got to his office it was already almost ten o'clock. During his long walk he had made up his mind to haul in his fishing nets, now that it was all clear to him. No more games of mirrors.

"Cat, send Augello and Fazio to me."

"Isspecter Augello's not onna premisses."

"Then get me Fazio."

He decided not to tell Fazio anything about his meeting with the commissioner and Arquà. It would have been a waste of time and he didn't feel like wasting any more.

"What is it, Chief?"

"Listen, Fazio, I urgently need you to do two things for me. The first thing is that you have to find out, before the morning is over, how many cars Carlo Nicotra has and what their license plate numbers are."

"Where does Nicotra suddenly appear from?"

"He hasn't suddenly appeared. He's always been

around. You yourself mentioned his name, at the beginning of this story."

"You're right. But I can't figure out how he's involved in this and to what degree."

"Fazio, you surprise me. He's the one who had Arturo Tallarita and Liliana murdered."

"But why?"

"Ever heard of Romeo and Juliet?"

"Yeah, I saw the movie once."

"Romeo and Juliet belonged to two rival families, which made their love impossible."

"Come on, Chief, what's Nicotra got to do with a story of impossible love?"

"But didn't you tell me that Tallarita's father dealt drugs for Nicotra? You could therefore consider Nicotra as the head of one of the two families."

Fazio thought about this for a moment.

"All right," he said. "But what does he care if Arturo has a lover? From the north, to boot? Why wouldn't he want the two to be together?"

"But that's what I'm trying to tell you. Because Liliana belonged to another family."

"Chief, what family are you talking about? I repeat, not only are they from way out of town and have no friends, but Liliana's husband is a computer representative!"

"Or so it seemed."

Fazio balked.

"He's not?"

"Let's say it was a good cover. In fact, he may even have been one for a while, but then . . ."

"So what did he do, then?"

"He dealt drugs. Big time. He was given the task of taking over Nicotra's circuit, replacing him little by little until he could push him out."

"But how do you know this?"

"I've given it a lot of thought. Then, at a certain point, I wanted proof. And I got it."

"How?"

"By opening up a computer and printer that were still in the Lombardos' house. They didn't work. They were simply containers for cocaine."

Fazio's eyes opened wide.

"But Lombardo couldn't have been acting alone! And anyway, he's not even from around here! What could he possibly know about the local drug circuit?"

"In my opinion, he was most likely hired by the Cuffaros, who have been supplanted in the drug business by the Sinagras for a while now. He wasn't acting alone; I'm sure the Cuffaros were behind him. And they brought Lombardo in from the outside. You'll see—if we manage to arrest him, he'll turn out to be a big-time specialist in the field."

"I think I'm beginning to understand."

"When Nicotra discovered that Arturo had a thing going with Liliana, he must have got really worried that the kid might reveal some important secrets to his lover, stuff about his organizational system that Liliana would then tell her husband."

"So why not have him killed right away?"

"He can't, because he's concerned about how Tallarita senior, who's in jail, will react. It's possible the father would take revenge by collaborating in earnest with Narcotics. It's a kind of boomerang, really."

"How?"

"Because Nicotra himself started the rumor of his collaboration when he wanted to throw us off the scent of the bombs. So what does he do? He goes and talks to Arturo's mother, warning her that her son is going with a woman who could bring real harm to him, but then nothing happens."

"So he sends someone to vandalize her car," Fazio continued.

"Right you are. But in this case, too, no results. So he has Liliana shot at when she's in the car with me, but they miss. Same with the scoop, which was supposed to have driven a wedge between Arturo and Liliana, but that fails, too. Then at some point Arturo begins to understand Nicotra's intentions and suggests to her that she try to get everyone to think that she's my lover. But Nicotra knows that the two are still seeing each other. So he gets more serious. First he kidnaps Arturo, then Liliana, as she's trying to flee. Then he kills Arturo and—"

"Excuse me for interrupting, but why did he wait so long to kill Liliana?"

"Maybe he thought he could use her to put pressure on Lombardo. But apparently the guy didn't give a fuck about his wife."

"But why kill her in her own house?"

"To try to have the murder pinned on me. Nicotra wanted revenge for the failed scoop."

"And what about the bombs?"

"Nicotra had those planted to let Lombardo know that he'd been unmasked and that it'd be best if he moved to another neighborhood."

Fazio had no more questions.

"All right," he said, "I'll go and find out about those cars."

"Wait. The other thing I want you to do is talk to whoever's in charge and ask for permission to speak with Tallarita senior in prison. I'll need it for this afternoon. And by the way, was Signora Tallarita ever informed about the death of her son?"

"Of course. His sister came down from Palermo to identify the body."

An hour later Fazio came back and informed him that Carlo Nicotra had three cars. One was a Mercedes with the license plate GI 866 CP.

"Nicotra's fucked," Montalbano said to Fazio, who only gave him a bewildered look.

The inspector then started searching through the papers in his jacket pocket.

At last he found the scrap with Japico's cell phone number written on it.

He dialed it.

"Montalbano here."

"What can I do for you, Inspector?"

"I need to talk to you."

"I'm in town."

"Could you come to the station?"

"When?"

"As soon as possible."

"I'm right in the neighborhood. I'll be there in five minutes."

Fazio looked at him questioningly.

"This young man saw two cars at the drinking trough in Spinoccia before one of them caught fire. He took down the license plate numbers, but without the letters, only the numbers, so he could play them at Lotto. One was Liliana's Suzuki; the other was a big car that we now know was a Mercedes. Carlo Nicotra's Mercedes."

Fazio was confused.

"What's wrong? Doesn't make sense to you?"

"What I'm wondering is how can someone like Nicotra go in his own car to the place where somebody's about to be murdered? Why would he do that without taking the slightest precaution?"

"Because these people are morons who think they're omnipotent. Like some of our politicians. And they fuck up time and again."

Catarella rang to tell them as how there was summon called Imbilicato on the premisses . . .

Japico Indelicato was smiling.

"Is everything all right, Inspector?"

"Did your number win?"

"Nah."

"Well, it won for me."

"How's that, Inspector?"

"Was the license plate of the big car you saw in the rearview mirror by any chance GI 866 CP?"

Japico slapped his forehead.

"That's it! How did I ever forget it?"

"Why do you say that?"

"Because GI are the initials of Giovanni Indelicato, who's my father, and CP is for Carmela Pirro, who's my mother."

The tern had paid off.

"Now, Signor Indelicato, I want you to give me a straight answer."

"Okay."

"Would you be willing to testify, now, in my presence, and later, in a court of law, that that was the car you saw at the drinking trough in Spinoccia, and that you saw it there with another car, the one that was later set on fire?"

"Of course. Why would that be a problem?"

"Because the car belongs to a Mafia boss."

"I don't care who it belongs to, I'll say what I saw."

"Thank you. Fazio, get ready to type the declaration."

After Japico left, Fazio commented:

"There should be more young people like that!"

"There are, there are," said Montalbano.

"So what do we do now?" Fazio asked.

"I'm gonna go eat. If in the meantime you get permission to talk with Tallarita, ring me at Enzo's."

At Enzo's the TV was on and tuned in to TeleVigàta.

"Shall I turn it off or leave it on?" Enzo asked him.

"Leave it on."

"What can I get you?"

"I should keep to light stuff. I have a lot to do this afternoon."

"Tell you what. No antipasti, just first and second courses."

As the inspector was eating a dish of *pasta alla carrettiera*, Ragonese's face appeared on the TV screen. The newsman spoke at great length about some legislation passed by the regional government concerning the fishing industry, and not until the end of his report did he say:

Concerning the widespread recent reports about the possible involvement of a well-known local personality in the murder of Liliana Lombardo, a development we duly broadcast here at TeleVigàta, the Office of the Commissioner of Police of Montelusa has issued a statement asserting that all such reports are entirely without foundation and that the investigation of the crime still remains in the hands of Chief Inspector Salvo Montalbano of the Vigàta Police. Have a good day.

Old Ragonese seemed to be taking it a little hard. But Mr. C'mishner had kept his word, and Montalbano at least had to give him credit for that.

He was paying the bill when Fazio rang him on his cell phone. Before answering, he made sure there were no other clients within earshot.

"I can get you a consultation with Tallarita tomorrow morning at nine."

Montalbano spoke softly.

"All right. For now, though, don't leave the office, because I'm about to go to Tommaseo and ask him for an arrest warrant for Nicotra. And I'll have it sent to you; that way you can go and get him for me immediately. I want to talk to the guy before taking him to the prosecutor. Got that?"

"Got it."

He hung up and called Tommaseo's office.

"Can you see me in about half an hour?"

"Come."

As he'd expected, Tommaseo put up some resistance to issuing the arrest warrant.

"Well, only one witness . . ."

And the inspector had to thank the Lord that there was even one! In the past there wouldn't have been any.

"But we may have conclusive proof."

"And what would that be?"

"In addition to the arrest warrant, I want you to order the confiscation of all of Nicotra's cars. Especially the Mercedes."

"Why?"

"Because I'm absolutely certain that Liliana Lombardo was taken to the house in which she was murdered in the trunk of that Mercedes. A careful examination by Forensics should come up with, say, some of the victim's hair. The body's still in the morgue, so it wouldn't be hard to make a comparison."

In the end, Tommaseo let himself be talked into it, and then sent a copy of the warrant to Fazio.

Justice was on the move. But Montalbano wasn't convinced that justice would, in the end, do itself justice. It would encounter many and unceasing obstacles along the way: lawyers paid their weight in gold, honorable parliamentarians who owed their seats in government to the Mafia and had to repay the debt, some judges a bit less courageous than others, and a truckload of false testimonies in favor of the defendant . . .

But there might still be a way to screw Nicotra once and for all . . .

After leaving Tommaseo's office, the inspector went for a half-hour walk to allow Fazio time to do what he had to do; then he got into his car and headed for the studios of the Free Channel.

He parked, got out, and went in.

"How nice to see you!" said Zito's secretary.

"It's nice to see you, too. You're fresh as a rose. Is Nicolò in?"

"Yes, he's in his office."

Nicolò was writing. As soon as he saw Montalbano, he got up.

"What a lovely surprise! I watched Ragonese's report. Everything taken care of?"

"Everything."

"So much the better. You need something?"

"Yes. I want you to interview me and broadcast it this evening."

"At your service. Interview you about what?"

"Wait just a second. Can I make a phone call?"

"Of course."

He called Fazio on the cell phone.

"What point are we at?"

"We're taking him to the station."

"Did he put up any resistance?"

"No, he wasn't expecting it."

"How did he react?"

"He said he wants his lawyer."

"He'll have to wait till I get there. Oh, and do me a favor and inform Tommaseo that he'll have Nicotra standing before him in about two hours."

Montalbano hung up and turned towards Zito.

"I'm giving you exclusive rights to the scoop: I've just had Carlo Nicotra arrested for double homicide."

"Holy shit!" said Nicolò, jumping out of his chair. "Nicotra's the number two of the Sinagra clan! That's a blockbuster! Give me some of the details."

Montalbano filled him in. Then he said:

"So, are you going to interview me or not?"

"Yes, but I'm going to reveal the news of the arrest first, and separately."

"Do whatever you like."

▬▬▬

"Inspector Montalbano, could you please tell us how you arrived at the decision to request a warrant for the arrest of Carlo Nicotra?"

"Well, as you know, during a preliminary investigation we are required to maintain secrecy on many points, so I'll just limit myself to saying that it was Nicotra himself who took me by the hand and led me to the solution of the case."

"Really? Could you give me a better sense of how he did that?"

"Certainly. Nicotra made such a string of mistakes that at first I almost couldn't believe it. I actually thought they were red herrings to throw me off the scent."

"Could you give us a couple of examples?"

"Well, he made an anonymous telephone call to a well-known journalist and made no effort to camouflage his very recognizable voice, and he went personally, in his own Mercedes, to the killing of Arturo Tallarita, not bothering to mask the license plate . . . These blunders were so gross that I wonder how his bosses can still have faith in such a wreck of a man."

"And what, in your opinion—provided you're allowed to tell us—what was the motive behind these two savage murders?"

"Well, Arturo Tallarita fell in love with the married Liliana Lombardo, who was also in love with him. And

their affair did not go down well with Nicotra. He did everything in his power to separate the two lovers— wrecking the engine of Signora Lombardo's car, trying even to have her shot, but the bullet missed. . . .

"Finally, in exasperation, he had both of them murdered in particularly cruel fashion. Inexplicable behavior. Or perhaps it can be explained, since at first he was only trying to get the woman. But such matters are beyond my competence."

"Are you trying to tell me Nicotra saw Signora Lombardo as a rival?"

"I repeat that is not within my competence to plumb the depths of the soul of a multiple murderer like Carlo Nicotra, but that is one of the possible explanations."

"How is it that there has been no news of Signora Lombardo's husband?"

"I don't know the answer to that. But since he works as the representative of a large computer company—and in fact there are still a few computers at his house—and travels a great deal, it's possible he still doesn't know what happened to his wife. We're hoping he comes forward as soon as possible."

He'd taken care of Nicotra. After saying what he said, it was unlikely the Sinagras would pull out all the stops to defend him. They had no more use now for Nicotra; indeed, they might even consider him a risk. Better to let him rot in the bowels of some prison. And he'd quite purposely thrown down the trump card by insinuating that Nicotra might prefer boys, a sin that his bosses would never forgive.

After the interview, he phoned Fazio again.

"I'll be back at the office in half an hour at the most. I want Mimì Augello there, too, so I can explain to him how we narrowed things down to Carlo Nicotra. He'll be the one to escort him to the prosecutor's office. And have a television with a DVD player ready on my desk."

Then, turning to Zito:

"Could you make me a copy of the interview?"

He was parking in the station's lot when Fazio, who had apparently been waiting for him, came and opened the car door.

"What is it?"

"Zaccaria the lawyer's here. He's in the waiting room. He was obviously sent by the Sinagras."

Michele Zaccaria, elected to Parliament in the majority party by a landslide in the last elections, was the top lawyer of the Sinagra family. He was very good at his job, one of the best. He'd come just in the nick of time.

"Did you find a video monitor and a DVD player?"

"Yup."

They went into the office. Montalbano took a video disk out of his pocket and handed it to Fazio.

"See if this works."

"What is it?"

"An interview I did with Zito."

"And why do you want us to see it?"

"You'll understand as soon as you see it."

They set up the chairs in such a way that Augello, Fazio, Nicotra, and the defense counsel Zaccaria could watch the show. Montalbano himself wasn't interested in the video. He wanted to enjoy another, much more interesting show, the one put on by Nicotra's and Zaccaria's faces as they watched the interview.

"Okay, bring 'em all in."

18

Carlo Nicotra, a tiny man of about sixty with fine features and extremely well groomed, a sort of cross between a chief physician and a ministerial division head, was known to be a cold-blooded fish. They said he never, under any circumstance, lost his cool. Indeed he didn't look the least bit uncomfortable and acted as if he were among friends.

Montalbano and Zaccaria greeted each other with a barely perceptible nod of the head. After everyone had sat down, the inspector turned to the lawyer and began to speak.

"Let me start by saying that there will be no interrogation at this time. I consider it unnecessary. However, before turning the suspect over to the public prosecutor, I feel duty bound to have him listen to an interview I gave today that will be broadcast on the evening news tonight and on subsequent news reports."

Nicotra, who was certainly surprised but didn't let it

show, limited himself to whispering something in his counsel's ear, to which the lawyer responded by doing the same.

"Does either of you have any objections to the viewing?" Montalbano asked.

"None whatsoever," the lawyer replied.

The inspector gestured to Fazio to begin.

When he heard himself being called a "wreck," Nicotra's face turned as red as a beet and he squirmed in his chair. But at the point in the video where Montalbano insinuated that he might be in love with Arturo Tallarita, he suddenly emitted a sort of lionlike roar, stood up, and lunged at the inspector, but Fazio grabbed him by the shoulders and forced him to sit back down.

"Can we go back a ways?" the lawyer asked, cool as a cucumber. "In all the confusion I missed something."

He seemed quite interested. Nicotra, on the other hand, kept his eyes fixed on the floor.

"All right," Montalbano said when it was over. "Now Inspector Augello is going to accompany the suspect to the prosecutor's office. Have a good day."

"Just a moment," said the lawyer Zaccaria. "Since I have another urgent engagement, an associate of mine, Barrister Cusumano, will accompany Signor Nicotra to the prosecutor's office in my place. So I ask you please, Inspector, to wait for my colleague to get here before sending these men away. All right?"

"All right," said Montalbano.

"Thank you, and good-bye," said Zaccaria, practically running out of the room.

"Fazio, take him to a holding cell and then come back."

As soon as he was alone with Augello, the inspector started laughing. Mimì looked at him darkly.

"What's so funny? I didn't see the point of the interview."

"You didn't either? Let's wait for Fazio to return, and then I'll explain."

Fazio returned.

"Now I get it!" he exclaimed.

"Then if you would be so kind as to share some of your wisdom with a poor ignoramus . . ." said Augello, getting more and more irritated.

"Mimì," said Montalbano. "What can be gathered from this interview is, first of all, that I come off as a first-class asshole who still doesn't have a fucking clue as to the true motive of the double murder—that is, drugs. And that's why the good lawyer dashed off to inform the Sinagras of my ignorance. Their next move will be to show that I'm right, and that Nicotra has always been gay. Is that clear now?"

"When you put it that way, yes, it's clear. But for what purpose?"

"Wait. Secondly, in the interview I also blurted out that there were still a few of Lombardo's computers and printers at the house. As Fazio must have told you, those are simply containers for cocaine. But I pretended not to know that. And by way of conclusion, I would bet the family jewels that that house is going to be mobbed tonight."

"I'm beginning to understand," said Augello. "You're setting a trap for Lombardo."

"Lombardo's at the top of the list. Knowing that Nicotra's behind bars, he'll feel safe and will rush back to recover the merchandise before the court sequesters everything in the house. But the trap's not only for him."

"So for who else, then?"

"For the Sinagras, of course. I would say they're practically obligated to get those computers and printers out of there without wasting another minute. That is, before I discover what's inside them. Because if I never find out, then they're completely out of the picture. But if I do, they're in it up to their necks. Got it now?"

"Got it," said Augello.

"So what's the plan?" asked Fazio.

"Simple," said the inspector. "The interview will be aired three times this evening: at eight, at ten, and at midnight. I'm one hundred percent convinced that Lombardo is lurking nearby. But he won't show up before two a.m., when the traffic on the main road becomes scarce. And the Sinagras will also come out around the same time. I want two teams. One on the sea side of the house under your command, Mimì, and one on the land side, directed by Fazio. You'll go on duty at midnight."

"And what about you?" asked Mimì.

"Around the same time, I'll go into the Lombardo house and lie in wait in the small room with the computers."

"Wait a second," said Mimì. "Let's make sure we're on the same page. When am I supposed to intervene?"

"If it's Lombardo, let him enter the house and I'll deal with him. If, on the other hand, it's the Sinagras' men, arrest them the moment they set foot inside," said Montalbano.

"But how will we tell it's them?" asked Mimì. "It's not as if they'll be wearing name tags."

"Look, Lombardo has the keys to the house and will be alone. He'll surely come in through the front door. The Sinagras, on the other hand, will send at least two men, and they'll try to enter through the back, on the beach side, where it's safer. They'll have to remove a few of the planks to enter through the boarded-up French door."

"And how will we communicate to you when someone is approaching?" asked Fazio.

"I'll bring a cell phone. Set it so that it doesn't ring but just vibrates. That'll be enough for me," said the inspector.

At that moment Catarella rang to announce the arrival of the lawyer Musulmano. Who naturally was Cusumano.

"I'm going home to Marinella. You can call me, if necessary, up until midnight."

"Bring your weapon with you," Fazio advised him before leaving the room.

The first thing the inspector did when he got home was to turn on the television. The Free Channel was airing his interview. Then he switched to TeleVigàta. Pippo Ragonese was in the process of commenting on the news item of the day, the arrest of Carlo Nicotra. Poor Zito hadn't managed to scoop anyone with the story. Apparently the Sinagras had wasted no time informing Tele-Vigàta of the new development.

> . . . *it was probably his insane passion that drove Nicotra to murder the two lovers with such ferocity. Arturo Tallarita was brought to the place of his execution in the trunk of Nicotra's own Mercedes, taken out, goat-tied with a thin steel chain, and put in the backseat of Lombardo's Suzuki, which was then drenched in gasoline and set on fire. Nicotra wanted to enjoy the horrific spectacle to the bitter end, as the young man struggled to free himself of the chain, merely killing himself slowly while the flames attacked his flesh . . . What words can describe such terrible agony? We will do everything possible to keep you informed of this atrocity . . .*

The inspector prayed that Signora Tallarita wasn't watching TV and turned it off. Everything was going as planned. The Sinagras had abandoned Nicotra to his destiny. And therefore, in order to keep what Ragonese called the "insane passion" thesis alive and safe from any evidence to the contrary, they had to get their hands on the computers and printers in the Lombardo house.

He went and opened the refrigerator. There was nothing. In the oven, however, he found a casserole of *pasta 'ncasciata* and a nice platter of fried shrimp and calamari. A special treat.

He set the table on the veranda and enjoyed the beautiful evening and good food, taking his time with everything.

Later, he cleared the table, washed up, and rang Livia.

"Since I have to go out later—"

"Where are you going?"

The whole thing was too complicated to explain.

"To the movies."

"With whom?"

There was a note of alarm in her voice. Surely she thought he was going out with a woman.

"You skipped a line of dialogue."

"I don't understand."

"I'll explain. If somebody says they're going to the movies, the next line is supposed to be: 'To see what?' 'With whom,' if anything, would be the line you'd say after that."

"I don't care what film you're going to see; I care about who you're going with."

"I'm going by myself."

"I don't believe you."

A spat was inevitable.

━━━━

At half past ten, Mimì Augello rang.

"I'm on my way back to Vigàta. Tommaseo interrogated Nicotra and locked him up. He'll resume the questioning tomorrow morning at nine. Any news at your end?"

"Not a thing."

"All right, then I'll go directly to the station. See you tonight, Salvo."

Montalbano sat down in the armchair and started watching a film he'd seen before and liked.

The second time around he liked it even more, and he was so engrossed in it that the ringing of the telephone made him start.

It was Fazio.

"Everything okay, Chief? My team's heading out to Marinella now."

The inspector looked at his watch. Fifteen minutes to midnight.

"What about Augello?"

"He's already left, about twenty minutes ago. He worked something out with the Harbor Office—got them to give him a motorized dinghy."

━━━━

It was time for Montalbano to get moving as well. He took a good long shower, then put on just a pair of jeans and a shirt. It was too hot to wear anything else. He made a pot of coffee and filled a thermos with it. He took his pistol, stuck it in his waistband, then grabbed his keys and a flashlight. He looked around for his cell phone but couldn't find it. He started cursing the saints. At last he found it under a newspaper, put it in his shirt pocket, and went out of the house with the thermos in his hand. This time there was no need to wear gloves.

After removing the seals from the front door, he opened it, went inside, and closed the door behind him, hoping no one had seen him from the main road. Once inside, he opened the bedroom window, climbed over the sill, and jumped into the yard. He must have landed badly on his left foot, because he felt a sharp pain in his ankle.

He ran limping to the front door, put the seals back on, climbed back through the window, closed it, went and opened the little room, entered, then locked the door from the inside with a skeleton key.

Lombardo mustn't suspect anything.

The small room was the same as the last time he'd been in it. The computers and printers were still in their places.

He sat down on the little bed, turned off the flashlight, and started massaging his foot in the dark, thinking bitterly that his days as an athlete were behind him.

He'd dozed off without realizing it, despite all the coffee he'd drunk. Sitting still on a cot in the darkness and total silence induced sleep. The vibration of his cell phone thus had the effect of an electrical charge on him, almost making him fall off the bed. He turned the flashlight on for a split second: it was two thirty. He grabbed his pistol, cocked it, and kept his eyes fixed and ears pricked in the direction of the door, which he couldn't see.

Then he heard someone walking softly in the hallway. The man hadn't made a sound coming in. Or at least Montalbano hadn't heard anything. The door handle turned with a sort of squeak, but the door didn't open, since it was locked.

Then something incredible happened.

Somebody knocked lightly with his knuckles, and a polite voice said:

"Inspector Montalbano, would you please open the door for me? I lost the key for this room."

Montalbano froze, paralyzed. The voice, which had a slight Veneto accent, continued.

"I assure you I'm unarmed," it said.

What had the cleaning woman said? That Lombardo always carried a revolver. The inspector didn't trust him. Moving about in the dark, he went and flattened himself against the wall beside the door; then, holding the pistol in his left hand, he reached out with his right and, still keeping himself covered, stuck the key in the door and turned it, standing immediately aside.

"You can come in."

He held the shining flashlight in one hand and the gun in the other.

The door opened slowly and Adriano Lombardo appeared. He had his hands up.

He was tall, blond, and good-looking. And perfectly calm.

"How did you know I was here?" Montalbano asked him.

"No offense, but your trap was too naïve."

"So why did you come?"

"Simple. To turn myself in. I was abandoned some time ago by the Cuffaros, and now the Sinagras' men are after me. I'm better off in jail. I haven't killed anyone, after all."

"Why do you say the Cuffaros abandoned you?"

"They immediately realized that the plan to take over the Sinagras' drug circuit was too difficult, and so they left me on my own."

It was an absurd situation. They were chatting like two old acquaintances in a café.

At that moment they heard a sudden racket in the area of the veranda. It must have been the Sinagras' men breaking down the planks. Then they heard a voice say:

"So where the fuck is this little room?"

Heavy footsteps were heard in the dining room. But

why wasn't Mimì intervening? Montalbano went out into the hallway, saw the beam of a flashlight coming towards him, and fired. The flashlight went out, and a voice cried:

"Turì, take cover!"

There must have been at least two of them. Montalbano and Lombardo couldn't let themselves be trapped in the room. The inspector flopped belly down on the floor and fired another shot. But what the hell was Mimì waiting for? Inside the room, meanwhile, Lombardo had moved the bed and was busy doing something he couldn't figure out. The Sinagras' men were on the move, perhaps preparing to mount an assault.

Then a burst of machine-gun fire came suddenly from the dining room. Too high, but Montalbano realized he was lost. The man with the machine gun took a step forward and let fly another burst. Montalbano raised his pistol and . . .

A sharp, clean shot rang out behind him. The machine gun fell to the floor, and the man who a second before had Montalbano's fate in his hands did the same without a cry.

"Turì! Turì!" the second man called.

There was no reply. Montalbano distinctly heard his hurried footsteps. The man was running away. The inspector turned around and shone the flashlight. Adriano Lombardo was smiling and holding a precision rifle.

"Put the weapon down."

"Of course."

Outside, meanwhile, they heard cries of "Stop! Police!" and a few gunshots.

"Where was it?"

"I kept it hidden in that room. There are some removable bricks under the bed."

Montalbano had a flash.

"Was it you who fired at your wife when she was in the car with me?"

"Yes, but she wasn't my wife. She was just someone I'd brought along who I thought might be useful to me. But I would never have killed her. I'm an excellent marksman."

"So why did you shoot at her?"

"To win your support against the Sinagras, Inspector. And by the way, it was I who told Liliana to try to seduce you. I was sure you would suspect Nicotra and act accordingly, getting him out of my way. Instead you did nothing. Why?"

"I'll tell you some other time," said Montalbano.

They heard Mimì calling from the beach.

"Salvo! You can come out now."

They went out. By the light of the flashlights, Montalbano noticed that Mimì was completely drenched. A short distance away, two uniformed cops were restraining someone.

"We nabbed him. He said you killed his friend."

"I didn't. The man standing here, Adriano Lombardo, did. Why'd you guys get here so late?"

"The outboard motor on the dinghy broke down. We rowed for a while, then dove into the water and swam."

Fazio meanwhile had shown up with two other policemen.

"Mimì, take Lombardo into custody as well and put him in a holding cell. We'll talk about what to do with him tomorrow. You, Fazio, had better report that I was in a firefight with one person killed. Then confiscate the computers and printers and take them to headquarters. I'm going home to bed. I feel a little tired."

He arrived at the station at eight thirty the next morning. He felt rested despite the fact that he had slept barely three hours.

"Fazio, I've got less than ten minutes. I have to be at Montelusa Prison at nine to talk with Tallarita. Bring me Lombardo and leave me alone with him."

Lombardo looked as if he hadn't gotten any sleep on the wooden plank in the holding cell. His clothes were in order. He just had a bit of stubble on his face.

"In a few minutes Inspector Fazio will escort you to the public prosecutor. I unfortunately have another engagement. But I hope to be able to come by midmorning. If you have any important revelations to make, please wait for me to get there. Do you have a lawyer?"

"No, but I want revenge on the Cuffaros. I have a lot to say about them."

"I imagined you would. I'll tell Augello to find you a good lawyer."

"Why are you so interested in me?"

"Because you saved my life. Which I'll tell the prosecutor. And also because . . ."

He stopped in time. But Lombardo smiled at him and finished his thought.

"Because you owe it to Liliana?"

Montalbano didn't reply.

He showed up at the prison gate ten minutes late. The chief guard told him to wait and started talking in a low voice into the telephone.

Then he called another guard and ordered him to escort the inspector to the prison warden.

What was this? He didn't have any time to waste.

"Look, I'm supposed to be having a consultation with—"

"I know, but the warden arranged it this way."

He knew this warden. His name was Luparelli and he was a perfectly respectable man though a pain in the ass when it came to protocol.

Montalbano found him agitated and in a bad mood.

"You won't be able to talk to Tallarita."

"Why not?"

"Something very serious happened. This morning in

the showers he slit Nicotra's throat with a knife. Nobody knows how he got the weapon."

"Did he kill him?"

"Yes. You see, yesterday he watched Ragonese's report on television, which went into all the gory details of his son's death, and so he avenged him. Afterwards, with the knife still in his hand, and threatening everybody around him, he started yelling that he wanted the Narcotics squad and he intended to turn state's witness. And so I called them, and they came and took him away."

He'd come all that way for nothing. But he'd achieved the result he wanted just the same. He'd planned to tell Tallarita about the terrible death his son had suffered, to trigger a reaction. But Ragonese had spared him the effort.

Leaving the prison, he got in his car and headed for the office of the public prosecutor, Tommaseo.

Where Lombardo was ready to take the Cuffaros to town.

It was a fine day indeed.

Author's Note

Unlike many other novels in the Montalbano series, this one did not originate from one or several news items. It's completely made up. I can therefore say with all the more conviction that all the character names, situations, and occurrences have no connection with actual events. Such things could occur, of course, and actually did, in the summer of 2010, after I'd written the novel. But that's another matter.

Notes

17 It was said that the Piedmontese were false and polite:
The Italians have a popular saying, according to which *Il Piemontese è falso e cortese*.

66 The military cops were responding: The carabinieri are a national police force and technically a branch of the military.

69 *"Nuttata persa e figlia fimmina":* A Sicilian expression that means "a lot of effort but nothing to show for it." The literal meaning is "a night wasted, and it's a girl," reflecting the culture's premium on male children.

103 the ACI: The Automobile Club d'Italia.

110 Buridan's ass: The dilemma, named after medieval French philosopher Jean Buridan (ca. 1300–ca. 1360), whereby a donkey, standing equidistant from a pail of water on one side and a bale of hay on the other, must die of hunger and thirst because it lacks the rational capacity to choose the one or the other.

147 *sartù di riso alla calabrisa:* A variant on a Neapolitan dish, *sartù di riso alla calabrese* belongs to the southern Italian tradition of *pasta al forno*, except that it uses rice instead. Like those baked pasta dishes, it features a great variety of ingredients, including pork, beef, peas, meatballs, eggs, sorpressata, tomato sauce, provolone cheese, pecorino cheese, bread crumbs, onions, and so on. When it is finished, it is removed from the casserole and looks rather like a large cake of rice. In Calabria it is often served as the main course on Fat Tuesday, at the start of Lent.

165 A proxy vendetta: The Italian term is *vendetta trasversale.* In Mafia language, this means taking revenge against somebody by attacking his family or friends.

186 cornuto: Italian for "cuckold."

196 "He was goat-tied": The Sicilian term is *incaprettato* (containing the word for goat, *capra*), and it refers to a particularly cruel method of execution used by the Mafia, where the victim is placed facedown, and then a rope (or in this case, a light chain) is looped around his neck and then tied to his feet, which are raised behind his back, as in hog-tying. Fatigue eventually forces him to lower his feet, strangling him in the process.

239 at the station for the temples: The fictional city of Montelusa is modeled after the real Sicilian city of Agrigento, outside of which stands the famous Valley of the Temples, a major ar-chaeological site of Sicilian Greek architecture. There are seven temples, all in the Doric style, mostly from the fifth century BC.

247 *pasta alla carrettiera:* A simple dish of pasta with a spicy tomato sauce containing a great deal of garlic, hot pepper, and parsley.

Notes by Stephen Sartarelli